The Gimlet Eye

James Roy was born in Trundle, NSW and spent much of his life as a missionary child in Papua New Guinea and Fiji. His books have garnered many awards over the years including various Premiers', CBCA, IBBY and Royal Blind Society Talking Book of the Year awards. He currently lives in the Blue Mountains with his wife Vicki, daughters April and Holly and dogs Otto and Rosie.

Quentaris – Quest of the Lost City

Book 1: *The Spell of Undoing*
by Paul Collins
Book 2: *The Equen Queen*
by Alyssa Brugman
Book 3: *The Gimlet Eye*
by James Roy

By James Roy

Hunting Elephants
Town
Problem Child
Queasy Rider
The Legend of Big Red
Ichabod Hart and the Lighthouse Mystery
Billy Mack's War
Captain Mack

THE GIMLET EYE
James Roy

First published by Ford Street Publishing, an imprint of
Hybrid Publishers, PO Box 52, Ormond VIC 3204

Melbourne Victoria Australia

© James Roy 2009

2 4 6 8 10 9 7 5 3 1

First published 2009

National Library of Australia
Cataloguing-in-Publication entry
Author: Roy, James, 1968–

Title: The Gimlet Eye / James Roy

ISBN: 9781876462772 (pbk.)

Subjects: Imaginary places--Juvenile fiction
Quests (Expeditions)--Juvenile fiction

Dewey Number: A823.3

Cover art by Les Petersen
Interior illustrations © Louise Prout
Cover and insert art © Grant Gittus Graphics
Series editors: Paul Collins and Michael Pryor
Consultant: Randal Flynn

Visit www.quentaris.com

Printing and quality control in China by
Tingleman Pty Ltd

Contents

For Tantan

PROLOGUE

The Archon was dying. In his palace, beside the Square of the People and in the shadow of the great mainmast and sails that towered over Quentaris, the old man lay breathing his last.

The room was silent, save for the deep, sighing, gasping breaths of the man who had spent so much of his life serving Quentaris. His nephew Florian Eftangeny sat by his side, his plump face devoid of emotion. It wasn't Florian's way to show anything as weak as sadness.

In fact, the only emotions he'd ever been known to show were anger, envy, bitterness, arrogance and occasionally fear. None of the good emotions, like love, or empathy, or gentleness.

'You may touch him, my lord,' the court physician said in a whisper.

Florian grunted. 'Why would I want to do that?'

'He's in pain, my lord. He might like you to hold his hand.'

Florian turned his head slightly. 'In pain, you say?'

'Yes, my lord.'

'Then *ease* it!' Spittle flew as Florian shouted at the physician. 'In the name of all that's magical, man, give him something to relieve him of it!'

The physician swallowed hard, gave a quick nod, and scurried out of the room.

'Melpeth,' Florian snapped, pressing his fingertips to his temples.

The servant lad came over, bowing his head low. 'Yes, my lord?'

'Melpeth, I'm still waiting for the magicians.'

'Yes, my lord,' Melpeth murmured, quickly backing away with his head still bowed. Then he too turned and scuttled out.

'Idiots,' Florian said. 'I'm surrounded by idiots.'

'Why do you even want the magicians

here?' asked a voice from the shadows that gathered amongst the wall hangings on the far side of the room. 'What do you think Stelka and her brood of gibberers are going to do for him now?'

'They need to see this, Janus,' Florian replied, flapping his hand towards the tiny, shrunken man in the bed. 'They need to see that it's gone too far now, even for them. They need to know that there's nothing that even they can do. That ...'

'That it's your turn?' Janus stepped forward into the light, eyes still hidden by the dark triangular shadows of his brow. 'Florian, I'm only saying this because I'm your friend. I wouldn't say this to just anyone.'

Florian looked up. 'What's that? What do you need to say to me?'

Janus walked across the cold marble floor on silent feet, stopped in front of Florian, and dropped to one knee. 'My lord,' he said. 'It is your time.'

Florian's eyes darted towards the Archon's face. 'Janus! He's not even dead yet!'

'Florian. You know that there is the power that is assumed, and the power that is taken, and they're not equal. They never have been, never will be.'

'Of course I know this – we studied the same texts,' Florian snapped.

'If your uncle dies now – if he simply stops breathing – you will assume great power. You'll be the leader of Quentaris ...'

'I get the feeling that you haven't quite finished that sentence,' Florian said.

'Indeed. But if you *take* that power, your grip will be that much the stronger. The prophecies are very clear, my friend. If he dies, you simply oversee. But if you act now, you *rule!*'

'I rule.' Florian bit his lip in thought as he glanced toward the door. 'So it must be now?'

'It must.'

'Very well,' Florian said at last. 'Watch the door.'

'You've made the right choice,' Janus said, standing and going to the door. 'All right, I'm standing guard.'

Florian stood, and reaching behind the Archon's head, he tugged at one of the thick pillows. He gripped it with both hands. 'Are you sure?'

'The prophecies,' Janus said.

'Yes, the prophecies.' He looked down at the face of his uncle. The old man's eyelids flickered open, and as their eyes suddenly met, the Archon's gaze widened, ever so slightly.

'Do it now, Florian, before the doctor comes back,' Janus prompted, his voice a hiss. 'There's no time to waste!'

'I know.' As Florian tightened his grip on the pillow, he saw the slightest shake of the Archon's head. Perhaps he even heard a tiny whisper escape the old man's thin, pale lips – a whisper that sounded like, 'Don't do this.'

'I must,' said Florian. 'I'm sorry, Uncle, but it has to be this way.'

Meanwhile, unseen in the darkest corner of the room, hidden by a tall-backed chair, a young boy watched with wide, terrified, disbelieving eyes. What he saw reached deep inside him, to the part of his mind that formed words – a part that was only now learning to speak freely again – and strangled it like a thickleberry vine entangling an ancient ruin.

A MOST STRANGE INVITATION

Tab Vidler sighed and dumped one last shovelful of dung into the bucket. It was like déjà vu. Here she was, a one-time Dung Brigader, who had become an apprentice magician, who was now back to shovelling animal waste into buckets. It didn't seem fair, even though working as a farmhand at the Nor'city Farm was a little less demeaning than traipsing around the streets picking up warm piles of animal droppings.

'When you're done there, you can get started on the stables,' called Bendo Lizac as he crossed the courtyard for the kitchen. 'The donkeys need more straw.'

'Yes sir,' Tab answered wearily. Then, as if for old times' sake, she closed her eyes and went probing with her mind for one of the donkeys. Something went *chink* in her head, and she was suddenly looking down at the floor of one of the stalls. A long, furry grey muzzle stretched before her field of vision.

>>>Forgive me<<< she whispered in her mind to the donkey, and she felt it give a mental shrug. This wasn't the first time she'd gone reaching in this way.

She directed the donkey to turn its head, and saw that there was ample straw in the corner of the stall. And in the next, and the next.

>>>Thank you, my friend<<< she told the donkey, who shrugged again.

'Why are you still standing there?' Bendo asked as he crossed back over the courtyard, biting the end off a boiled egg. 'I told you to give the donkeys more straw.'

'They've got plenty,' she replied.

Bendo paused, turned and walked towards her, slowly, menacingly. He stopped when their chests were almost touching, and glared down his nose at her. A couple of flecks of egg were stuck to his bottom lip. 'Listen, you, I don't pay you to talk back – I pay you to do as I say!' he snarled.

'Yes, sir, I'll do it straight away,' Tab murmured. 'Sorry.'

'Better.' Bendo turned and stomped away, and Tab sighed again.

'You don't pay me to talk back? No – you don't pay me at all,' she muttered.

'I heard that.'

'Sorry.'

Tab picked up the dung bucket and carried it over to the large pile in the corner of the yard. When its contents had been deposited, she headed into the stables. Even if she didn't top up the straw, she had to be seen to be doing as she was told.

The last few months had been … well, interesting. Since the Archon had died, so much had changed, and not just for Tab. Quentaris was hardly the same place any more. It was still floating in the sky, drifting almost aimlessly over forests, oceans, deserts, mountains. From time to time and without warning a vortex would appear, and the city would turn and sail straight for it, its vast sails cracking and flapping far above the rooftops. The swirling, black funnel of darkness would loom larger, and with barely enough time to get the animals inside to safety or to take the laundry in from the line, the shuddering and rumbling would begin. And a short time later, the landscape would have changed to different forests, oceans, deserts, mountains. Then the repairs around the city would begin again.

There had been a time when she was part of all of that, back before it became quite so random. As an apprentice magician, she had been close to the Navigators' Guild. She'd even come to count Chief Navigator Stelka as a friend, and had often been at the gatherings when the next vortex had been sought, found and entered. But since the Archon had died and his nephew Florian had taken over, there seemed little rhyme or reason to the vortexes they passed through, and the worlds into which they led.

But then, over time, and as the Navigators were demoted one by one, there did appear to be a logical explanation for the worlds to which they travelled. The thing was, Quentaris had become no better than the dreaded and despised Tolrush. Quentaris was now little more than a pirate city, sending out scouting parties, then raiding parties, before heading into the next vortex to do it again. Except no one that Tab or any of her friends spoke to seemed to agree with what was happening, so who was in the scouting parties? Who was following the orders of Florian?

Everyone Tab had grown to know and trust within the upper echelons of the Quentaran government had either been demoted, corrupted or in some cases, had simply vanished. Most of the magicians had disappeared. Their former leader Stelka was in a dungeon somewhere, charged with breaking some ancient law that had never been removed from the Constitution – something to do with pigs and sheep sharing a pen, or so it was rumoured. The former Quartermaster Dorissa and the other magicians had been exiled to a dark, haunted corner of the city, and Captain Verris hadn't been seen for months. Tab had enquired after him, and was given several different versions: a landward scouting expedition that had turned bad; an uprising in one of the rougher parts of the city that had led to several of the authorities dying, including Verris; one person had even whispered to Tab that he'd died of a broken heart after his favourite horse was lost overboard. All Tab knew was that even as a one-time pirate, Verris would never have approved of what the new Quentaris had become.

At least she still had her friends, she mused. Philmon's work as a skysailer was more hectic than ever, now that Quentaris was constantly plunging through vortexes. He complained about the number of repairs required, but as Tab always reminded him, at least he wasn't shovelling anything. Amelia, who had been well on her way to qualifying as a magician, was serving drinks in a tavern now, and Torby ... well, she still visited Torby from time to time, but he wasn't the same. He was a shell, still haunted by the effects of his torture at the hands of Krull and his Tolrushian henchmen. He'd seemed to improve for a while, after the equens had been to Quentaris, and had even begun to grow in confidence with his magic. But in the weeks and months following the death of the Archon, he'd worsened once more, and no one was quite sure why. Nowadays he lay in a never-ending state of staring awakedness on his bed at the end of a row in the Grendelmire Infirmary. He just lay there, day after day, occasionally twitching, but never speaking. With her friends, Tab would visit him when she could, but they always left wondering if he even knew who they were.

And then there was Fontagu. For a time, just before the Archon's death, Fontagu's star had been on the rise. His underhandedness forgotten or forgiven, perhaps both, he'd performed in several plays at the New Paragon, the rebuilt version of the famous old playhouse that had once held pride of place in the bustling eastern end of the city. The original Paragon had burnt to the ground during the battle with the Tolrushians. But it had been rebuilt and was, for a time, back better than ever.

Fontagu had been in his element. He'd starred in a number of plays, had directed one or two, and had even started writing his own. But then the Archon died, and the bottom fell out of Fontagu's world. It was a complete mystery to him, how someone so handsome, so damned *talented*, could go from the most celebrated Simesian actor of his age to a nobody, *twice*!

'I don't understand,' he'd said to Tab, often. 'Me! *Me!*'

'You were too close,' Tab replied on one of these occasions. 'All that business with the equens, and the herdsfolk – you were a part of all that. It's not your fault, though. Florian just wanted to clean out everyone who had anything to do with the old days.'

'A new broom?'

'Exactly.'

'Which is exactly what I need if I'm going to keep doing my job at the Flegis Arms. Sweeping! Me, sweeping the floor of some commoner's drinking hole! It's an outrage, Tab!'

'You could try being a bit more grateful.'

'Grateful?'

'Yes! Amelia didn't have to help you get a job at her tavern. She put in a good word for you, and now you've got work. If you think about it, you'll realise that it could be worse.'

'How?' Fontagu looked up at her with the most pathetic hang-dog expression. 'How could it be worse?'

'You could be locked away in a dungeon, like Stelka. Or exiled in Skulum Gate, like Dorissa and Moreon and Aylia and all those other magicians. Or you could be missing altogether, like Verris.'

Fontagu grunted. 'At least if you ask anyone where Stelka is, they can tell you. But ask anyone where that great thespian, that *arteur* Fontagu Wizroth the Third is, and they'll offer a one-word reply: "Who?"'

Tab had to smile then. Once her friend got into one of these moods, it was almost impossible to lift him out of it.

Tab chuckled to herself as she fluffed up a stack of straw in one of the stalls. If there was one thing that had never changed – would never change – in Quentaris, it was Fontagu.

'When you've done that, you can see to the shickins,' Bendo said from the door. 'They need fresh water. And check for eggs.'

'Yes, sir,' Tab replied. Then, once Bendo had left, she muttered, 'There'll be no eggs, you idiot – they're roosters.'

She picked up the water pail from near the pump and headed over to the shickin pen. A little larger than a turkey, and at least twice as ugly, the shickins had been taken during a recent raid. All sorts of weirdness came into Quentaris after these raids, and it was all very well for Florian, tucked safely away in his new palace. If anything dangerous or infectious was brought aboard, he'd get plenty of warning, mainly in the form of common Quentarans dropping dead. It had only happened a couple of times, but he hadn't seemed too bothered. In fact, he'd been entirely silent on the matter.

'Were there any eggs?' Bendo asked, peering into the pen.

'No, there weren't any eggs,' Tab replied. 'These shickins are ... not laying yet.'

Bendo scratched his head. 'I don't understand. I was told by that man at the market that they would be terrific layers.'

'You're right, it is weird,' Tab said. 'Give them time.'

'But how *much* time?' Bendo leaned forward and growled at the birds. 'Eggs out of you, or you'll end up in a broth.'

'You tell 'em, sir,' Tab said.

Bendo scowled at her, trying to work out whether she was mocking him. 'Yes, well,' he said at last. 'When you've finished with the shickins, you've got a visitor.'

'Who is it?'

'That lad who's always hanging around – the skysailor. Don't be too long. I'm watching you closely.'

'I'll be quick,' Tab replied, letting herself out of the pen and latching the gate. 'And I've heard that shickins lay better if you sing to them.'

'Really?'

'Oh yes, everyone knows that,' she said. Then she dropped the pail by the pump and ran to the gate at the far end of the courtyard.

'Hey, Tab,' said Philmon. 'Sorry to come here while you're working.'

'That's all right,' Tab replied, leaning around the

corner to see if Bendo was still trying to convince the shickin roosters to lay for him. He was. 'What is it?' she asked.

'It's Fontagu. I can't get him to speak.'

Tab's eyes narrowed. 'Fontagu? You can't get *Fontagu* to speak? No, you can't be serious.'

'I am serious. I saw him, in his room. I knocked, and he opened the door, and sat back down, but didn't say a word.'

'Has he just received bad news?' Tab asked. 'You know, really shocking news?'

'That's just the thing,' Philmon said. 'He looked happy. His eyes were ... It's so hard to explain, but he looked like he was very, very happy. But I couldn't get him to say a word, so I came to get you straight away. I thought you might know what to do.'

'Is he still there?'

'In his room? Yes. I told him I was coming to get you, and he seemed ... well, excited, I guess.'

Tab glanced around the corner again. Bendo was still crooning softly to the shickins, who seemed completely oblivious to his attentions.

'All right,' she said. 'Let's go and have a look at him.'

They made good time through the narrow streets, and soon reached the boarding house where Fontagu kept his lodgings. Tab took the steps three at a time, with Philmon close behind. 'Should I knock?' she asked.

'I think it's still open.'

Tab pushed the door, and it swung open with a small squeak. Over at his small desk in the corner sat Fontagu, with his back to the door. He didn't turn around, or even flinch as they came in.

'Fontagu, it's me,' Tab said gently. 'And Philmon. We came to see if you're all right.' She padded across the floor and rested her hand on Fontagu's shoulder. Still nothing. Then she looked at his face. Philmon had been right – he looked happy. He looked blissful. He seemed to be frozen in a state of delight.

'Fontagu?' she said again. 'What's going on?'

Slowly Fontagu turned his head, until his eyes were staring deep into hers. He dropped his hand to the desk, which was cluttered with paper and quills and empty ink jars, and picked up a piece of parchment, which he handed to Tab, without his eyes shifting from hers.

'What's this?' she asked, looking down at the

parchment. She saw the Supreme Crest at the very top. And below that, a letter written in the finest calligraphy. 'The writing's all curly. It looks like it's from Florian.'

'Really? What's it say?' Philmon asked.

'If you stop reading over my shoulder I'll tell you,' she said. '"From Florian the Great, Supreme Ruler of Quentaris, Duke of Eftangeny, Lord Regent of the Western Skies, salutations. Herewith We order you, Fontagu Wizroth the Third, to present a play for Our pleasure and entertainment on the happy occasion of Our birthday. Any disinclination on your part will be looked upon by Us in a light most unseemly, and met with consequences most dire. You are ordered to present yourself at Our palace on the morrow, whereupon you shall accept Our most gracious invitation, and report upon the play which

shall glorify Our Person, and be forever remembered as a true and glorious portrayal of the Greatness that is Florian.""'

'Odd gods!' breathed Philmon. 'So it was bad news after all.'

'I know,' Tab said. 'You could never present a play that glorifies that sack of offal. Fontagu, what are you going to do?'

Fontagu's eyes were sparkling, and he was beginning to break into a grin. 'Do?' he said. '*Do*? I'm going to put on a play, of course!'

'But this is a death sentence,' said Tab, waving the letter in the air. 'Every royal command performance in the last year has ended up with at least one of the performers disappearing or dead, sometimes both!'

'That's right,' said Philmon. 'Please tell us you're not going to do this, Fontagu. The man's crazy! I mean, look at this letter! Supreme Ruler of this, Duke of that, the Greatness that is Florian ...'

Fontagu snatched the parchment away from her and stabbed at it with a long, bony finger. 'This is going to put me

back on the *map!*' he proclaimed. 'This is going to get me back in the daily bulletins!'

'Yes, in the obituary section,' Tab said. 'Fontagu, Philmon's right. If you agree to do this, you'll probably end up dead.'

Fontagu pushed back his chair and strode to the window. He stood there for a dramatic moment, with his chin raised, his fists on his hips, and his feet wide apart. 'My dear children, this is what actors live for!'

What they die for, more likely, Tab thought.

Fontagu went on. 'Actors dream of this. This! Unless you have ever trodden the boards, heard the hush of the crowd, the crescendo of applause, felt the warmth of the footlights against your face, you can never understand this feeling, this ...' – he turned suddenly to face them – '...this *rush* that comes of being wanted, being adored, being –'

'Doomed,' Tab said. 'Fontagu, you have to hide. You have to leave, now. Because I promise you, this can only end badly.'

'Maybe Skulum Gate would be a good place to hide for a while,' Philmon suggested.

Fontagu's face changed suddenly. His aura of aloofness had gone, and in its place was a flash of anger. 'Frankly, children, I'm insulted,' he said. 'I'm very hurt indeed that you don't think better of your friend Fontagu. Why, I was playing the part of Despero when this ... this so-called "ruler" was still a pup. I was taking three, four, five ovations a night at the original Paragon when Florian wasn't even thought of.' His eyes took on a far-off expression. 'I did a command performance for the Archon when he was still young, strong and knew what day it was.' His eyes returned to Tab and Philmon. 'So don't tell me that I can't pull this off. Don't tell me to run off and hide like a rat down in Skulum Gate with the witches.'

'They're not witches – they're magicians,' Tab said.

'Whatever. Just don't tell me that I can't please Florian the Great with my acting genius. I can, and I *will*!'

Tab and Philmon glanced at one another. They both knew that their chances of talking Fontagu down from this foolishness were very slim indeed.

'So, with that settled, there's no time to waste,' Fontagu said, striding to his desk and ruffling through his papers. 'And I know just the thing. Where is it?'

'What are you looking for?' Tab asked.

He ignored her. 'I know it's here somewhere ... Yes, here it is!' he declared in triumph, producing a collection of loosely bound pages from below a pile of documents and holding it aloft. 'This is the thing that will please Florian, not to mention bring all those silver moons rolling back in. It doesn't get any better than this, children – a royal command performance of a great classic. Oh, the fame! The fortune! The glory! The —'

'State funeral,' Tab muttered.

'Right, that's it!' Fontagu snapped, spreading his arms wide and herding Tab and Philmon towards the door. 'Out! If you can't be more supportive ...'

'Oh, come on, Fontagu,' Tab protested. 'We're just saying ...'

'No. No! You're being terribly, terribly disrespectful, and I won't stand for it. I've always suspected that you were laughing at me behind your hands, but this confirms it for me. Out. Out!' He held the door open.

Philmon smiled and shook his head in disbelief. 'Come on, Tab, let's go.'

'I do think that's best,' Fontagu said, pointing his nose at the ceiling.

SMALL MINDS

'You're in trouble,' said Freya, the pale young girl who worked with Tab at Nor'city Farm. 'Bendo's furious.'

'I had to check on a friend.' Tab looked around the complex of courtyards, stables and outbuildings that made up the farm. 'Where is he?'

'That's what he was wondering about you.'

'Oh, he won't hurt me,' Tab said. 'He wouldn't dare. We've got an understanding.'

'Vidler!' Bendo shouted. He was striding across the courtyard towards her, his jaw set tight. 'Where were you?'

'Somewhere else. But I'm back now.'

'I could thrash you,' Bendo sneered.

'You could, but you won't.'

'Hmm,' he grunted.

Tab smiled. Her only proper magical skill was the ability to inhabit the minds of animals, but Bendo didn't need to know that. All he knew was that she'd once been an apprentice magician. She liked that he was still a little wary of what she might do to him, or turn him into.

'Just ... just go and finish your chores,' he muttered in the end.

'Thank you, sir,' Tab chirped, wandering off to do the last of her jobs before the sun sank behind the high dry-stone wall of the farm.

After she'd finished, and tidied away her tools, she went to her tiny bedchamber, which was situated in a draughty annex off the end of the stables. Four farmhands lived in that annex, each with their own stall. Tab suspected that these stalls had once held animals, but that at some time long before she had come to live at Nor'city Farm, someone had nailed wall panels to the rails. A hessian sack hung down in front of each open doorway like a rough curtain, so there was a little more privacy now than the original inhabitants would have enjoyed, but it was still pretty harsh accommodation. Certainly a lot more spartan than the last place in which she'd lived, sharing modest but clean and breezy apartments with several other apprentice magicians.

Now she sat on her straw-sack mattress, closed her eyes and went reaching for one of her usual animal friends. She'd become a lot more practised at mind-melding, and in addition to the animals at the farm, with whom she would sometimes meld just to pass the time, there were a number of other, more important creatures she used for far nobler purposes.

As she focused her mind, a number of voices and awarenesses flickered through her consciousness. It was a little like walking past a busy schoolyard, and hearing different shouts, cries and conversations drift in and out, at times coming to the foreground, then drifting away to be background hubbub while other voices pushed forward.

But it wasn't just voices in her mind's ear. It was also

a series of shadows and flickers of light in her mind's eye, as if she were trying to see a wild creature behind a shrub, just tiny movements through gaps between leaves, never  the whole, but definitely parts.

She shuddered, and pushed past the dog nosing about in a pile of rancid food scraps. It wasn't a dog she needed. The cat she sometimes used to spy on Bendo threatened to distract her, but she squeezed her eyes closed a little more tightly and carried on.

Then it was there. She felt her nose twitch, and pushed down the desire to scratch at imaginary whiskers. In her mind she saw darkness, and a gap of light, in the shape of a rough triangle. She'd found Rat.

>>>Rat, it's just me<<< she said, and the nose-twitching stopped as Rat felt her. >>>Thanks for letting me in again<<<

Rat replied, in a very clumsy way. >>>Did I even have a choice?<<< it asked, or at least that was how Tab interpreted it.

>>>I need to talk to Stelka<<< she explained. >>>Please go forward<<<

Rat did as she'd asked, scurrying towards the gap

of light. As it got closer it stopped, and poked its nose out. Through its eyes, Tab looked around.

Over on the far side of the cell, sitting at a rather ramshackle table, was Stelka. All her jewels and various decorations were now gone, taken by Florian, or someone answering to him. Her hair, once her pride, now hung in long, lank tresses, and her silk gown was soiled, scuffed and stained, and coming apart at some of the seams.

>>>Speak<<< Tab ordered the rat. >>>Please<<<

From partly within her own throat, and partly within the rat's, Tab heard a shrill screech. Stelka looked up from her writing, stared at the wall before her, then turned to look directly at Rat. 'Oh, is it her?' she asked. 'Just a moment.'

Tab saw her close her eyes, while a look of enormous concentration tightened her face. Then, a moment or two later, she heard Stelka's voice, stilted and uncertain, contained within the mind of Rat.

>>>Good you come<<< Stelka's voice said.

>>>I need to talk to you<<< Tab said. >>>I need to know what I should do<<<

There was a pause. Stelka was new to mind-melding. Everything she knew, Tab had taught her within the confines of the tiny mind of this most accommodating rodent. So it was quite normal for the replies to come back rather twisted and dificult to understand, and slowly.

>>>What you need know?<<< Stelka finally asked.

>>>Fontagu has been asked to perform a play for Florian<<<

The answer was almost instant. >>>No, bad idea<<<

>>>I know – that's what I told him<<<

>>>When he do play?<<<

>>>He's going to the palace tomorrow. I'm worried that he's going to say or do something stupid<<<

>>>Like going to palace?<<< Stelka's voice said, and even through the fuzzy translation, Tab could hear her suppressing her laughter.

>>>What should I do?<<<

>>>Go with<<< Stelka's voice said.

>>>Go with him? What good would that do?<<<

>>>Find out him's plan. Then can fix<<<

>>>Keep an eye on him, you mean<<<

>>>Yes. Stelka must go now<<<

Like a tiny pull on the hair at the side of her head, Tab felt Stelka's mind-meld separate from hers. Through the eyes of Rat she saw that one of the troll jailers had entered the corridor that ran beside the cells, and was talking to her friend.

>>>Thank you, Rat<<< Tab said. >>>That's all for today<<< She could have waited for Stelka to be finished with the jailer, but the conversations they had were only possible through the grudging goodwill of the rat, and she didn't want to push her luck. With a soft sigh, she separated her own mind from Rat's, and was suddenly aware once more of the stall she called home.

She stood then, and shook her head, trying to clear the fine cobwebs of mind-meld that always hung around after these 'conversations' with Stelka. Then, pulling her cloak around her shoulders, she slipped under her curtain, trotted silently to the end of the annex and, with practised movements, climbed the rough brick wall like a spider, using small jutting ledges for foot- and handholds. She reached the narrow gap in the corner where the two walls and the roof converged, and then, with no more sound than a quick exhale, she had squeezed through the gap and was dropping silently down into a Quentaran back alley.

She had a message to convey.

* * *

Tab slipped through the backstreets, taking care to stick to the shadows. Even someone like her, with better than average magic skills, wasn't completely safe at night – not since everything had changed. She didn't wish to be spotted by anyone who wanted to try to rob her, even with nothing to steal, and she didn't fancy being taken by the ear and dragged back to face Bendo.

So she slunk around the ends of buildings, ducked into culverts and behind barrels, hid under the cover of shadows while late-night drunks staggered by, or guards laughed and swore on street corners. And she certainly made a point of giving Skulum Gate a wide berth. There might have been old friends in there, but she still had little desire to run into any of them. Not now.

One of Philmon's fellow sky-sailors opened the little flap in the middle of the door of their quarters. 'Yes?'

'It's me, Tab.'

'It's very late.'

'I need to see Philmon.'

'It's very late.'

'So you said. Can I see him? Please? I won't take very long.'

'Wait there.'

The little flap slapped shut, and Tab stood just a little closer to the door while she waited.

Finally the door rattled, and opened slightly. 'Tab! What are you doing here?' Philmon asked, holding the door open.

'I had to see you. I had to tell you – I'm going to

go up to the palace with Fontagu tomorrow.'

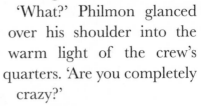

'What?' Philmon glanced over his shoulder into the warm light of the crew's quarters. 'Are you completely crazy?'

'I have to go with him. Stelka said –'

'*Stelka*? It's all very well for *her*, Tab – she's already locked up!'

'I know. But I have to do this. He needs me. After all, he's a friend.'

Philmon rolled his eyes. 'Some friend. Have you forgotten that it was Fontagu who got Quentaris into this whole city-in-the-sky mess to begin with? Are you sure this is wise?'

'Not so loud! And no, I'm not sure at all,' Tab admitted. 'But I'm going to do it anyway. Fontagu needs my support. Anyway, what's the worst that could happen?'

'I don't want to think too hard about that,' Philmon sighed.

'We don't have to say anything. We'll just hover in the background –'

Philmon's eyes narrowed. 'Hold on, Tab, what

did you just say? We'll just hover in the background? We? As in, you and me?'

Tab swallowed hard, and gave him a quick, nervous smile. 'I *could* go on my own. Or I could go with a friend.'

'I thought Fontagu was your friend.'

'*Another* friend?' she suggested. 'Come on, Philmon, if Florian planned to do anything to us, he'd have done it long before now. He doesn't see us as any kind of threat. If he did, he'd have locked up me and Amelia along with Stelka. Or even worse, we'd be in Skulum Gate.'

'I guess ...' Philmon said.

'So, will we meet near Fontagu's place just before noon tomorrow?'

Philmon shook his head slightly and heaved a sigh. 'I can't believe I'm saying this ... Sure, why not?'

Tab grinned, and squeezed his arm. 'I knew you wouldn't let me down. Well, I'd better get back. If I'm caught out of my chamber, Bendo won't be happy.'

'Bendo's going to be the least of your problems after tomorrow,' Philmon muttered.

FONTAGU GOES IT ALONE

The following morning Tab awoke early and quickly got to work. Then, when she'd finished her chores, she did some more, simply so Bendo wouldn't be able to shout at her for being lazy. At about mid-morning, she found Bendo and told him that she had to go out for a while.

'Go out? Where?' he asked suspiciously.

'I've got an errand I have to run,' she explained. Then, before he could say a word, she added, 'I've finished everything I had to do.'

'The water troughs?'

'Done.'

'The chaff-bags?'

'Full.'

'Even the donkeys' bags?'

'*Especially* the donkeys' bags.'

'The stables?'

'Cleaned. And they've got fresh straw too, before you ask.'

'I wasn't going to ... Oh, good then. The shickins?'

'Fed and cleaned.'

'Any eggs yet?'

Tab shook her head. 'Still no eggs.'

Bendo turned away, his brow furrowed. 'I don't understand why they're not laying,' he muttered, shaking his head.

Smiling to herself, Tab took the opportunity to slip out the gate of the farm and into the bustle of people in the street outside.

The thoroughfares were particularly crowded today, so it took longer than usual to reach Fontagu's boarding house. When she arrived, Philmon was waiting on the opposite side of the street, sitting on a low step. He seemed annoyed. 'Where have you been?' he asked, standing up.

'I've been coming,' she said. 'There were so many people. Has Fontagu already left?'

'Yes! He went a few minutes ago.'

'Did he see you?'

'No, I don't think so. He had his head in one of his play-scripts. He was definitely being all "actor-ish",' Philmon added with a flourish.

Tab rolled her eyes and groaned. 'That's all we need – Fontagu getting all high and mighty and full of himself.'

'Is he ever any other way?'

'I guess not. Come on, we should catch up to him. Rooftop?'

Philmon nodded. 'Rooftop.'

Moments later they were on the roof of Fontagu's boarding house, having shimmied up a drainpipe, scampered along a thin wall, vaulted over a parapet and climbed another pipe. There weren't too many places in Quentaris they couldn't go in this way. In fact, on one occasion they'd managed to get from the port side of the city to the starboard without their feet touching the ground once. Sure, they'd come to a couple of dead ends on some of the taller buildings and had had to double back to find a new route, and it had taken the better part of a day to do it, but they'd succeeded in the end.

Now, they made their way to the rooftops and headed aft, towards the mainmast and the palace beyond it. They stayed as close as possible to the street which took the most direct route to the palace, looking out for the tall, flamboyant Fontagu.

'What was he wearing?' Tab asked Philmon.

'The usual. Hat with feather, velvet cape.'

'The red one?'

'No, the purple one.'

'Oh!' said Tab, surprised. 'He is serious, isn't he? The *purple* one? Well, at least we know what we're looking for.'

They continued along the rooftops, still searching the crowds below for the white-feathered hat and the purple cape with the gold braiding around the edge. Finally, just disappearing around the corner of

a house, they spotted Fontagu, striding along, script in hand.

'There he is!' said Tab, pointing. Then she dropped off the edge of the roof, landing softly on a narrow balcony below, startling a reclining old man who was snoozing there in the sun.

Philmon followed her over the edge, only stopping long enough to apologise to the old man.

'Fontagu!' Tab shouted, running across the street, through a group of children, and past a slightly nervy donkey.

Fontagu turned around and gaped in surprise. 'Tab?' he said as she jogged up, breathing hard. 'And Philmon? I say, children, to what do you owe this great honour?'

'Don't you mean –' Tab began.

'I know what I meant,' Fontagu said. 'Why are you here? I'm on my way to the Archon's palace at Florian the Great's behest.'

'We know. That's why we're here. We think we should come with you.'

Fontagu shook his head furiously. 'Absolutely not! It's out of the question! Why, the very idea!'

'But why not?'

'Why *not*? Let me ask you a question in return, my dear young friend. What could you possibly expect to achieve by coming along?'

'We can look out for you,' said Tab. 'We don't think you know what you're getting yourself in for.'

Fontagu laughed, loud and booming, and it made Tab scowl. She hated being looked down on, almost as much as she hated being laughed at.

'I'm serious, Fontagu.'

'Oh, I'm sure you are, but I simply can't let you come along.'

'I told you this was a foolish idea,' Philmon said to Tab.

'We won't be in any danger, if we just hang back.'

Fontagu suddenly looked rather stern. 'Oh, I'm not thinking about you being in danger. I just don't think I can be seen with you. I mean, look at yourselves, you in particular, Tab. You look like you've just been cleaning out the stables of some farm animal.'

'Yes, well ...' Tab began.

'And you, Philmon – what have you come as?'

'I'm just dressed the same way I usually am,' Philmon replied, looking a little hurt.

Fontagu sniffed. 'Indeed. Whereas I ... I am *resplendent*!' He held up one of his long, bony hands, and tilted his chin back. 'No, I'm afraid I must be most emphatic on this. I simply cannot allow you to come in with me.'

'Told you,' Philmon muttered, taking Tab by the elbow. 'Let's go.'

'Good advice,' Fontagu said. 'I'm sorry, children, but this is grown-ups' business. Grown-ups' business for which I do not intend to be late. Goodbye.' And with that said, he turned his back and strode away up the hill.

'So ...' said Philmon.

'This isn't over,' Tab replied.

'Come on, Tab, it is over,' Philmon said, gently pulling her away.

Tab yanked her arm free. 'Philmon, tell me, what is the stupidest animal you know of?'

'Stupidest?' He shrugged. 'I don't know – a rat?'

'No, rats are clever and cunning.'

'Sheep?'

'Well ... kind of. But no. Here, watch this.' She strode forward to where Jilka the street vendor was selling loaves of bread. A crowd of pigeons had gathered around, waiting for crumbs, and they only moved out of the way as someone approached the stall to buy something.

'Hi, Jilka,' she said. 'Good sales today?'

'So-so, Tab,' Jilka replied.

'Can you spare a crumb for an old friend?'

'I can give you a whole loaf if you like.' Jilka took a flat roll from the top of the pile and tossed it to Tab. 'On the house.'

'Thanks, Jilka,' she said, tearing off a hunk and putting it into her mouth. As the crumbs fell around her feet, the pigeons, which were as bold as house pets, squabbled around her feet, pecking for the tiniest morsels.

Tab pulled off a small piece of bread and tossed it out into the middle of the street, and the pigeons turned and flapped after it. One at the front of the pack got there first, snatched up the bread in its beak, and flew away to eat in peace.

'So?' said Philmon.

'Now watch,' Tab said, pulling off another chunk and pretending to throw it. As she raised her arm, most of the pigeons rose into the air and tried to hover there, anticipating another offering of bread. When nothing came their way, they began to resettle on the ground.

'Now, watch *this*.' Tab bent and picked up a small, pale coloured pebble. She lobbed it gently away, and the pigeons spun as one and raced to be first to what they thought was more bread. One of them skidded up to the pebble, grabbed it with its beak, then dropped it suddenly.

'See? Stupid.'

'Fine, pigeons are stupid,' Philmon agreed. 'So?'

'So we're going to get into that palace after all. Come on.'

And she turned and trotted off up the hill towards the palace, with Philmon in confused pursuit.

* * *

'I don't understand,' Philmon said.

Tab said nothing. Instead she frowned and looked around the Square of the People. Behind them was a newish fountain, and the statue in the middle was of Florian. It was quite a gruesome statue – it depicted a rather slim Florian holding up the head of some enemy or another, and the water in the fountain poured from the neck of the corpse at his feet. It was supposed to show the bravery and greatness of Florian, but pretty much everyone in Quentaris knew that Florian had never done anything brave in his life.

The fountain was of less interest to Tab than what was in front of them, however. Tall and imposing, the aft-side wall of the newest part of the palace was nearing completion. Some of the scaffolding was still in place, and was dotted with various workmen, who were busily adding gaudy gargoyles and decorations to the palace in time for Florian's birthday. Over the last year the palace had gone from a grand but austere building to a huge, obscene monument to the huge, obscene ego of Florian. There was no end in sight.

'Tab,' Philmon said.

'Shh,' Tab replied. 'I'm thinking.'

'That guard over there is watching us.'

'Let him watch. We're not doing anything ... yet.'

'He doesn't look Quentaran.'

'He's probably not. He'll be one of those new guards that came aboard a couple of months ago.'

'Oh yes, I remember. Was that –'

'Shush! I'm thinking,' Tab said. 'Now, the new Great Hall is in there, isn't it?' she said.

'Yes, behind that wall with all the windows.'

'Excellent.' She smiled at Philmon. 'I think I have a plan.'

Tab sat at the base of the fountain and leaned against it. She couldn't bring herself to look at the statue. Besides, she wasn't taking in the sights.

Her eyes were squeezed shut, as Philmon sat nearby to keep watch, and a pigeon on the other side of the square stopped pecking at the cracks in the pavement and stared into space with a glazed expression.

>>>Don't be alarmed<<< Tab was saying within the pigeon's tiny mind. She was trying to say it in a cooing type of mental voice. Maybe she was succeeding, or maybe the pigeon was a particularly unquestioning specimen. Either way, she felt the bird open its mind to her, just a little.

>>>Good<<< Tab went on. >>>Now, there's something I need you to do<<<

A moment later the pigeon rose into the air with a whirring coo, and flew up and up, past the scaffolding to one of the open panes at the top of the ornate window that provided so much natural light into the throne room of Florian the Great.

FONTAGU IN TROUBLE ... AGAIN

The thin-faced man in the velvet skullcap stopped in front of Fontagu and gave a very small, very unconvincing bow. 'The Emperor will see you now.'

'I should think so, too,' Fontagu replied, slipping his long fingers under the gold-braid edge of his cape and giving it a flick. 'Do you know how long I've been waiting here?'

'You'd best show a little less of the superior attitude, if you know what's good for you,' the man in the skullcap advised. 'The Emperor prefers to be the most important person in any room.'

'Indeed.' Fontagu's throat was dry as he tried to swallow. 'Of course. Thank you.'

The man nodded to one of the palace guards, who swung open the huge carved doors that led into Florian's great chamber.

Fontagu gasped. It was a large room, full of shiny, ornate things, and people in expensive looking clothes, with shiny, ornate things hanging from them.

At the far end of the room, under the huge window, and flanked by a couple of statue-still guards, was Florian. His throne was made of marble, with a high carved back and a velvet seat-cushion. He lolled against one of the arms, his beady little eyes even more lost in his face than ever. The life of an emperor was a good one, especially the food he could ask for at any time, day or night. Evidently he asked for it day *and* night.

The man in the skullcap cleared his throat and announced the entry of Fontagu in his streaky voice. 'Fontagu Wizroth, my lord.'

'The Third,' Fontagu muttered.

The man ignored Fontagu's correction, choosing instead to bow low and back away to the side of the room.

Rather than speaking to Fontagu, Florian turned

his head to address the tall young man who stood, hands clasped, beside the throne. 'Janus, who's this again?' he murmured.

'This is Fontagu, the actor.' Janus said the word 'actor' with all the distaste of a contagious disease.

'Oh yes, I remember.' Florian sat up a little higher. 'Come a little nearer, Actor,' he said, in a louder voice.

Fontagu took another step closer, then dropped to one knee and bowed his head, just as he'd been instructed to do. 'My lord, it is my truly great, great honour.'

'Yes, yes, get up,' Florian said, waving his hand lazily. 'So, presumably you received Our missive?'

'Your what? I mean, I don't understand, my lord.'

'Our missive. Our message. Our letter. Oh, never mind. You must have got it – you're here now, aren't you? So, what did you make of it?'

'Your letter? Oh, I thought it was very good.'

Florian raised one eyebrow. 'Good?'

'Well worded. And the calligraphy was quite exquisite – did you do it yourself?'

'What?' Florian blustered. 'Of course I didn't do it myself! I've got ... I mean, We have scribes to do that kind of thing!'

'Of course you do,' Fontagu replied quickly. 'I'm sorry, I didn't mean to suggest –'

'Oh, do shut up,' Florian sighed. 'So, are you going to do it or not?'

'The play? Yes, of course – it would be a great honour.'

'Yes, indeed it would. And you're to spare no expense, do you hear?'

Fontagu bowed his head. 'None shall be spared, my lord. Is there someone I should talk to about the production budget?'

Florian frowned. 'I fear you misunderstand Us, Actor. *You* are to spare no expense.'

'Um ... Oh!' Fontagu suddenly burst out laughing. 'Oh, you mean my money! Of course, how silly of me!'

Janus put his hand to his mouth and disguised a laugh with a cough. 'You didn't think the Emperor was going to spend his own money on a birthday gift for himself, did you?'

'No! No, definitely not,' stammered Fontagu.

Tiredly, Florian raised one hand, and Fontagu fell silent. 'All right, you're wasting Our time. Tell me, Actor, what play have you chosen to perform for Us?'

Fontagu reached under his cloak and took out his manuscript. 'If it please my lord, I would be honoured to present for your edification my original production of *The Gimlet Eye*.'

'*The Gimlet Eye*, indeed?' Florian replied. 'We've seen that once before.'

'All respect, my lord, but you've never seen it done like Fontagu Wizroth the Third shall do it.'

'We'll see,' Florian grunted.

'Is that the script there?' Janus asked.

'Yes, sir.'

'Bring it to me,' Janus said, reaching out his hand, and the man in the skullcap hurried over, took the script from Fontagu and carried it to Janus.

'Um ... that's my only copy,' Fontagu protested.

Janus flicked through a couple of the pages. 'Very well,' he said after a moment, handing the script back to the servant, who returned it to Fontagu.

'We're done with this one,' Florian said with a tired wave of his hand.

'All right, Actor, go back to where you lodge,' Janus said. 'You'll hear from us in due course.'

'Thank you,' Fontagu said, bowing low. 'Thank you, my lord. Thank you everyone.'

Florian said nothing. He was somewhat distracted by the pigeon that had flown from its perch at the top of the large window behind him, swooped down into the throne room and, with perfect accuracy, dropped a small, runny spatter of white onto his shoulder.

* * *

With a quiet little thought of thanks, Tab extracted her mind from that of the pigeon. 'He's all right,' she told Philmon. Then she laughed.

'What's so funny?' Philmon asked.

'The pigeon – it left a little present for Florian. Right here,' she added, patting her shoulder.

'You made it do that?'

She smiled. 'I might have.'

'You're terrible, Tab,' Philmon said, breaking into a grin as well. 'So what happened? Did your trick with the pigeon work? Did you get a good look? Could you hear anything?'

'I saw everything, and I heard everything. He's doing a play, like he said. He's doing *The Gimlet Eye*.'

'*The Gimlet Eye*?'

'Yes. I remember Stelka used to talk about it from time to time. It's famous. In fact, I think I might have seen it once, with some of the other magicians. It was very long,' she added. 'I quite possibly fell asleep in the middle of Act Five.'

Philmon coughed. '*Five*? How many acts are there?'

Tab shrugged. 'I'm not actually sure. Six, maybe. I was asleep.'

'What's it even about?'

'It's one of those hero plays. You know, big scary monster thing roaming the land, terrorising the little people, until the hero stops it with some heroic act. Or something,' she added. 'Like I say, it's all a bit hazy.'

'Huh,' said Philmon. 'And I bet I can guess who the hero is going to be.' He stopped walking, puffed out his chest and slipped the end of his right hand inside the opening of his shirt. He tried to deepen his voice, which made it squeak and crack. 'It is I, Lord

Florian the Heroic, come to slay the ... What's the monster called?'

'The Gimlet Eye is the name of the monster. It uses its gaze to kill, or something.'

'And that's the play he's doing?'

'Yes.'

Philmon sniffed. 'Well, at least he's not dead. Yet.'

They hurried around the end of the palace towards the main front gate. With his hat and his cape, it didn't take them long to spot Fontagu, who was walking as quickly as his long legs could carry him.

'Thank the gods he's not running,' Philmon said.

'He'd never let anyone see him run,' replied Tab. 'How undignified!'

'He's definitely in a hurry, though,' said Philmon.

They jogged after him and, after pushing through the crowds near the palace and in the streets nearby, they finally caught up near the Old Tree Guesthouse.

'Fontagu! Hold up a minute,' Tab called, but he didn't appear to have heard her. He just carried on walking.

'Fontagu!' she called again. 'Font –' Her voice caught in her throat as a short, red-headed man stepped out of a doorway, and straight into the path of Fontagu, who took a sudden, uncertain backward step.

Judging by his broad shoulders and his hefty arms, the red-headed man had once been powerful. Much of that bulk had now softened, and following the laws of age and gravity, had transformed into a heavy gut. Even so, he still formed enough of an imposing figure to intimidate Fontagu.

'Who is that?' Philmon said.

'Just wait,' Tab replied, reaching out and holding Philmon back by the arm. 'Let's see what this is all about.'

'We can't hear what they're saying anyway.'

'Just wait,' Tab said again.

She was glad of that decision a moment later, when they saw the red-headed man step behind Fontagu, pinning his arm behind him. A flash of fear flickered across Fontagu's face, and as he was half-guided,

51

half-pushed into the doorway, Tab saw the glint of something shiny held against the small of his back.

'Now what do you suppose *that's* all about?' Philmon wondered aloud.

'Have you ever seen that man before? Because I'm sure I haven't,' Tab said.

Philmon shook his head.

'Huh,' Tab remarked to herself, turning to look behind them. 'What do you think we should do – follow them?'

'No need,' Philmon replied, as Fontagu reappeared, staggering slightly as he stepped down onto the pavement. His face was pale and his eyes wide as he glanced up and down the street, before setting off towards home. A moment later the red-headed man appeared as well. He too looked furtively up and down before limping up the hill towards Tab and Philmon, who did their best to melt into the crowd as he hurried past.

'What was that smell?' Tab said when he'd gone.

'Tigerplums,' Philmon replied. 'He was eating one.'

'Really? Why?'

'Some people like them.'

'Yes, crazy people.'

'Didn't you see the colour of his mouth? All stained yellow.'

'I didn't see – I was too busy trying not to vomit from the smell. It stinks worse than Vlod's spoiled boingy deer meat. Come on,' Tab said, and they ran down the hill in pursuit of Fontagu.

They caught up with him a couple of streets later. He'd been making very good time.

'Fontagu!' Tab panted as they reached him.

He spun around, his hand to his chest. Then the back of his hand went to his forehead. For a moment, Tab wondered if he was about to pass out. 'Oh Tab, must you startle a chap so? You know my disposition is delicate!'

'Yes, I'm sure it is, especially after you've been held up at knife point.'

'Whatever are you talking about, my dear child?'

'We saw you,' Philmon said. 'We saw that man with you.'

'Yes, that stinky, stinky man. Who was he?' asked Tab. 'And what did he want?'

Fontagu gave a forced laugh. 'Oh, *that*? That was nothing! That was just a ... a fellow actor, a thespian such as I. We were practising a scene.' He tried to smile.

Tab and Philmon simply frowned at him. 'Do you always rehearse in the middle of the street?' Philmon asked. 'Or in dark doorways?'

'Come on, Fontagu, we're not complete idiots,' Tab said.

Fontagu slumped a little. 'You're right, of course. He wasn't a colleague.'

'So who was he?'

Fontagu's usual demeanour was already starting to return. He flicked back his cape, adopted his dramatic wide-legged stance. 'You know, children, you don't have to know everything about my affairs. I am, after all, a grown-up.'

'We know,' Tab replied. 'It's just –'

'So don't be so nosy! Goodness me, you'd think that you were my sainted parents, the way you follow me around, constantly spying on me!'

'Did he have anything to do with your appointment at the court?' Tab asked.

'Or *The Gimlet Eye*?' Philmon added.

For a moment Fontagu was completely lost for words. It was something they very rarely saw. '*The Gimlet* ... How would you know about *The Gimlet Eye*? You *have* been spying on me!'

Neither Tab nor Philmon felt that they were in a position to disagree. 'It's because we worry about you,' Tab explained.

'Worry? About me? Why would you worry about me?'

Tab began to count off on her fingers as she spoke. 'You got ambushed by the Tolrushians, you betrayed Quentaris under so-called torture ...'

'It was torture!'

'... you smuggled the Equen Queen onto Quentaris ...'

'Not to mention that you stole an icefire gem and uttered a spell that sent Quentaris spinning into one vortex after the next,' Philmon said.

Fontagu's eyes flashed indignantly. 'You have never heard anyone accuse me of that!' he said defiantly.

'Only because the one person who saw you do it – me! – has never told any of the people she might have told.' Tab raised her arms high, pointing to the masts, rigging and great sails overhead. 'All of this is your doing, Fontagu. *All* of it! If anyone ever found out, they'd string you up in the Square of the People until the crows had pecked out your eyes, before throwing you to the scavenjaws.'

Fontagu winced. 'Don't say that. Please.'

'All I'm saying is that you haven't exactly been the perfect citizen up to now, so we worry about what you might get up to next. Or who might catch up with you,' she added.

Fontagu's chin was crumpling as he fought back tears. 'I do appreciate your concern, children, most sincerely I do. I am ever so touched. But you must trust me when I say that everything is under control. And with that said, I must take my leave. I have a great deal of preparation to ... to prepare. Yes, that's right, to prepare. So goodbye now.'

He turned then, and with a clumsy flourish of his cape he strode away. But his stride lacked some of its usual arrogance, as if some of his pride had leaked out of a small rupture in his side.

'"Trust me", he says,' Philmon muttered. 'I wouldn't trust that man as far as I could spit.'

'Did you notice anything missing?' Tab said.

'Like what? Tab? Where are you going?' He jogged after Tab, who had turned and was striding up the hill, back towards the palace.

'Did you notice anything missing?' Tab repeated

when he'd caught up to her. 'What was Fontagu carrying when he left the palace?'

'Um ... just his script.'

'And did he have it just then?'

Philmon frowned as he tried to remember. 'No, I don't think so.'

'So either he dropped his script, or Red-head took it. And I doubt that he'd drop something so precious. And did you notice how Fontagu managed to avoid telling us how he knew Red-head?'

'So where are we going now?'

'We're going after Red-head, obviously.'

'What are you going to say to him?'

Tab stopped and regarded Philmon for a long moment. 'I'm going to ask him why he was so mean to our friend Fontagu,' she said sarcastically. 'Honestly, Philmon, you must think that I'm quite the idiot.'

'I just wondered.'

'All I'm going to do is follow him.'

'Can I come?'

'I'd be disappointed if you didn't.'

INTENTIONAL TOURISTS

Tab and Philmon ran. Red-head was out of sight, but they were well practised at spotting particular people in a crowd, and before too long they saw him, limping, but limping quickly.

'I bet he's going to the palace,' Philmon said.

'Of course he is. The only thing is, I didn't see him there when I was mind-melding with that pigeon.'

'That doesn't mean anything. He might have been in another room.'

They followed Red-head at a safe distance, and eventually they saw that Philmon had been right. The man strode confidently − if slightly lop-sidedly − to the guards who stood at the front gate of the palace. He nodded to them in a very familiar manner, before simply strolling in.

'I knew it!' said Philmon.

'Congratulations,' Tab replied. 'Come on, follow my lead.' And without giving Philmon a chance to respond or refuse, she wandered over to one of the guards at the gate.

The soldier regarded them with a wary look. 'What does you want?' he asked in a strange, clipped accent.

'Oh no, we're perfectly all right,' said Tab. She looked up at the front gate of the palace and whistled in awe.

The guard shook his head. 'No, you no all right. You leaving, is what you are.'

'But we're tourists,' Tab replied.

'You no tourists,' the guard argued. 'They no have tourists in Quentaris since before the Spell of the Undoing.'

'If we weren't tourists, we'd know that already, wouldn't we?' Tab replied.

The guard frowned as he thought this over. It seemed like quite a lot for his brain to process. Then, suddenly, he lowered the tip of his halberd. 'You must think I a complete eediot,' he said.

'Oh no, not at all. We don't, do we?' Tab asked Philmon, who simply shook his head. 'So, you work here, do you?' she went on.

The guard said nothing. Instead, he patted his halberd.

'Of course,' Tab giggled. 'Silly me! So, you're a real palace guard! I suppose you'd know everyone here, probably?'

The guard shrugged. 'Pretty much.'

'You see, we're from out of town, like we said ...'

'Tourists,' Philmon interjected.

'Yes, and we thought we saw someone we knew.'

'Really?' The guard seemed rather disinterested. 'Who you think you know?'

'The man with the red hair who came through a couple of minutes ago. Short.'

'Fat,' said Philmon.

'And with a limp.'

'Hmm,' the guard replied.

'What was his name?' Tab enquired.

'I can no tell you that.'

'Was it Asro Mendeley?' she asked, plucking a random name out of her head.

The guard shook his head. 'That's no his name.'

'But I'm close, right? Asro Melando?'

'No.'

'No, no. Astrin Nando?' Tab clicked her fingers, then thumped her forehead with her fist. 'Oh, it's on the tip of my ... Argo Nadro –'

'Kalip Rendana.'

'Ah!' said Tab, slapping Philmon on the arm. 'Of course! Kalip Rendana!'

'I told you,' Philmon said. 'I told you it was Kalip Redondo!'

'Rendana,' Tab corrected him. 'And he's in charge of the kitchen in the palace, right?'

The guard sniggered. 'Hey,' he called to the other guard, who was standing on the opposite side of the wide stairs leading up to the huge main doors of the palace. 'This lot reckon Rendana work in the kitchen!'

The second guard spluttered with laughter. 'If he hear you say that he run you through with his leetle knife!'

'His little knife?' Tab asked.

'That's right. He a friend of Janus.'

Tab snapped her fingers. 'Of course! Yes, I remember now! Kalip Rendana! Yes, I saw him nod to you, though. Both of you! You know him. You actually know Kalip Rendana?'

'Sure I do,' said the first guard. 'We both do – him and me. Know him for years. We used to work for him, before we come aboard back when Quentaris was over Unja Ballis. He got us this job. Us and plenty our friends working in palace now. This job good job.'

'Aha!' Tab nodded. 'So you came aboard from Unja Ballis! I knew I'd never seen him before.'

The guard frowned. 'I thought you say you tourists. You not tourists at all! You both from Quentaris.'

Tab bit her bottom lip. 'Oops. Well thanks, it's been ... Bye!'

And she and Philmon turned and ran.

* * *

'Who is it?' Fontagu called, his voice sounding strained, and muffled through the heavy door.

'It's me, Tab.'

'Can't you children leave me alone?'

'It's just me,' Tab replied. 'I need to talk to you.'

'So you can insult me again?'

'It's not like that, Fontagu. Can't you just let me in?'

She heard him sigh. 'Hold on.' A moment later the door rattled and swung open. By the time the gap was wide enough to let Tab see inside, Fontagu had already crossed the room and was sitting at his crowded desk once more, and his quill was scratching away at a sheet of parchment. 'Close the door behind you,' she heard him mutter.

Tab did as he said, then stood inside the doorway. Ordinarily she'd have sat herself down without a second thought, but this time she could feel the tension thick in the air between them. 'Fontagu, I don't want to fight,' she said at last.

'What makes you think that I do?' he replied, without even glancing up. 'Look, Tab, unless you've got something new to say to me, you should just save your breath and go.'

'I do have something new to say. I know who the red-headed man is.'

Fontagu still hadn't looked in her direction, but she saw his pen stop moving. 'Even after we talked about this, you're still spying on me?'

'Fontagu, I told you, it was only because we care about you. We worry about you. Especially when we discover that the man who held you up in the street is actually working for Florian.'

Fontagu's eyebrows flickered in a tiny frown. 'What do you know about it?'

'I know that his name is Kalip Rendana, and he came aboard Quentaris back when we were over Unja Ballis, a couple of months back. And he works for Florian's man Janus.'

'Does he indeed?' said Fontagu, but his gulp gave him away.

'He does. And he took your play, didn't he?'

Fontagu finally broke down, dropping his forehead onto his desk and beginning to sob. 'Yes, he took my play – my only copy. He said there had to be changes made.'

'What kind of changes?'

'He wouldn't say. All he would tell me was that Janus was very keen to see one or two changes made to the original version of *The Gimlet Eye*.'

'Which he's going to make himself?'

'I think so. But no one was to know that Janus had made the changes. That's why he sent Rendana after me. The new parts are going to be a birthday surprise or something. It's all very hush-hush.'

'I don't understand,' Tab said. 'Why would Janus care so much about some play that he would take the time to make changes himself?'

Fontagu shrugged. He seemed so dejected. 'I don't suppose it matters now anyway. It won't be the same classic story any more.'

'No, I suppose not,' replied Tab, who was now deep in thought. 'But it does seem weird, doesn't it?'

* * *

Amelia yawned. 'I don't understand why it's so important,' she said.

Tab frowned. Perhaps a crowded tavern wasn't the best place to be discussing the big secrets of Quentaris. She gestured for Amelia to come closer. Then she lowered her voice. 'What's important is that Fontagu agreeing to do the play was already dangerous enough. But now this ... this person is threatening him. Fontagu thinks it's all about a birthday surprise, but I don't believe him. I mean, a knife? No, this Rendana's definitely threatening him.'

Amelia flipped her table-wiping cloth over her left shoulder and slipped into the seat opposite Tab. Then she leaned forward and took Tab's hands in hers. 'You've got a very short memory, Tab. Someone is threatening Fontagu – so what? Don't you remember all the things *he's* done?'

'I know.'

'He's got no conscience at all. None! He does whatever he likes, as long as it suits one person – him.'

'I know, but I think he's changed, Amelia.'

Amelia didn't seem convinced. 'Do you really? I don't know ...'

'Look, all I know is that Fontagu has been asked to put on a play for Florian –'

'A mistake,' said Amelia.

'True, but even so, he's going to do it. And now his play's been stolen.'

'Don't you mean borrowed?'

'I guess so.'

'Like I said, what does it matter? He'll get it back. Janus probably just wants to make sure that it's full of praise for the great and wondrous Florian. He's being a good subject.'

'Do you think?'

'I do. I also think you've been spending so much time with your actor friend that you're becoming as dramatic as he is.'

Tab bit her lip and thought about what Amelia had said. Maybe she was right. Maybe Fontagu was over-reacting, and maybe she was as well. It was quite possible that Rendana was simply the runner for Janus, who was just making sure that the play was perfectly suited to the big occasion of Florian's birthday. But even thinking this, she still came back to the knife ...

'You're probably right, Amelia,' Tab said at last, standing up. 'I'd better get back to the farm before Bendo notices I'm gone. Again.'

'Hunker down those shickins properly,' Amelia warned her. 'There's talk of another vortex tonight.'

Tab frowned. 'Another one? It's been less than a week since the last one!'

'I know. Something's going on.'

'You can say that again. Where do you hear this stuff, anyway?'

'Just chat in the tavern, mostly.'

'You haven't been heading down into Skulum Gate to get the inside information, have you?'

'As if I would! But you'd best go. It'll be getting dark soon, and you've got to walk right past Skulum Gate as it is. Then Bendo will be the least of your problems.'

* * *

Tab got the very strong impression that Bendo would have been a lot angrier with her if he hadn't been

thinking about the approaching vortex. 'Look over there,' he said, pointing towards the beetling purple-grey clouds building up to the west. 'We'll be there in an hour, maybe less.' He sighed. 'I'm so tired of this.'

'We'll get the goats in,' Tab said. 'It'll be all right.' Then she called to Freya, who was sweeping the pavement on the other side of the main courtyard. 'There's a vortex coming, Freya. We need to get the goats inside.'

'And don't forget to latch the lid of the straw-box,' Bendo said. 'I'll go and make sure that the shickins haven't laid any eggs yet. I'd hate for the first eggs they give us to be smashed all over the place in a vortex.'

Freya frowned. 'Eggs?' she asked Bendo.

'Yes, eggs.'

'From the shickins?'

'Yes, from the shickins!' he replied impatiently. 'So many questions, so little work!'

'But aren't they roosters, those ones?' said Freya.

Slowly Bendo turned his eyes towards Tab, who was trying to keep her growing grin under control. 'Roosters?'

Tab nodded.

'All of them?'

She nodded again.

'You knew this?'

'I suspected,' she said.

'And you didn't think to tell me?'

'You seemed so ... happy together, with the singing, and the patting ...'

'Goats!' Bendo shouted, his hands shaking, his face flushed. 'See to the goats, you revolting child! Both of you, before I lose my temper! And tie them up properly this time!'

As they scuttled away to see to the animals, Freya glanced up from under her eyebrows at Tab. '*Singing* to them? That's what you told him?'

Tab chuckled. 'Everyone needs a hobby. Mine is Bendo.'

* * *

Tucked up safely in her little sleeping-stall, Tab squeezed her eyes tightly closed and entered the mind of Rat. >>>Thank you<<< she said, gently coaxing the animal along the narrow tunnel towards Stelka's cell. She felt as if she was getting to know the creature. She wasn't sure if it was considered acceptable to feel like you were befriending the animal whose mind you occupied, but she had developed a gentle affection for the little creature, even if it almost certainly had yellow, protruding teeth and dozens of diseases.

A moment later she saw the triangle of brightness, and then stronger light as Rat poked its nose out. Stelka was standing at the far side of her cell, holding the bars and looking out into the corridor.

As she usually did, Tab made the rat squeal, and

at the shrill sound, Stelka turned around. 'Tab?' she asked, wiping her eyes.

With a gentle mental prod, Tab caused the rat to squeal again.

Over her shoulder, Stelka glanced further into the dark of the dungeon, before squatting down. Through Rat's eyes, Tab saw her bring her face closer. For a moment it felt as if the rat was flinching away and peparing to run. >>>Steady<<< Tab said.

Stelka closed her eyes then, and a moment later Tab felt her consciousness edging in alongside hers in the mind of Rat. >>>Is Tab?<<< she asked in her usual halting way.

>>>Yes it is<<< Tab replied. >>>I have to tell you something, Stelka. I followed Fontagu, like you suggested<<<

>>>What did happen?<<<

>>>He agreed to do a play. He's doing *The Gimlet Eye*<<<

>>>Very good story that one good choice<<< came the thought of Stelka.

>>>They took it away from him. They took his script<<<

>>>Who?<<<

>>>Do you know someone called Kalip Rendana?<<< Tab asked.

She felt Stelka hesitate, but it wasn't a hesitation that came of fear or uncertainty. It seemed to come of nothing more than Stelka thinking, turning the name over and over in her mind. Finally she had an answer. >>>I not know Kalip Rendana<<<

>>>He works for Janus, who works for Florian<<<

A shudder brushed past Tab's awareness. >>>He is bad man<<<

>>>Well yes, of course he is. We all hate Florian<<<

Somehow, through her next thought, Tab could feel Stelka's sudden flare of indignation. >>>Not Florian. Janus is bad man<<<

>>>He only works for Florian<<<

>>>Janus only works for Janus<<< Stelka answered.

>>>What should I do now?<<< Tab asked. >>>They took Fontagu's play<<<

>>>Do nothing<<< came the reply. >>>Wait

and watch. You are magician<<<

>>>What's that got to do with it?<<<

>>>Magician knows when to act. Go now. Not mind-talk too much for now<<<

>>>Are you all right?<<<

>>>Go now. Talk later. And be careful, friend Tab<<<

Tab felt Stelka's mind tear away like a piece of damp paper, and then she was alone in the mind of Rat. >>>Thank you again, little friend<<< she said, and as usual, the rat didn't seem even slightly put out.

Tab pulled away, and opened her eyes to see the inside of her little bed-stall. She lay back and listened to Freya humming quietly to herself in the next stall. Do nothing, Stelka had said. The former Chief Magician had never tried to hide her dislike of Fontagu, and had often tried to warn Tab that getting too close to him could lead to trouble. So was she now encouraging Tab to sit back and let Fontagu's nature lead him into the trouble that never seemed that far away?

Tab pursed her lips. How could she double-guess Stelka, who had nothing to gain from standing by and watching Fontagu destroy himself? She couldn't. She wouldn't. Tab had very few options anyway, so she would do exactly what Stelka had suggested. Nothing could be achieved by marching into the palace and demanding answers. So she would do

nothing, apart from waiting, and watching.

With these thoughts in her mind, and with the vortex-bells ringing high in the rigging, Tab pulled her blanket over herself and picked up her book.

A short time later, without too much fuss, the

journey through the vortex had come and gone. It all happened fairly quickly, and was barely even violent enough to make her stop reading. Sometimes going through a vortex led to buildings and walls falling down, and occasionally animals and even people being injured, sometimes even bits of the rigging came down in the streets. A few weeks before an entire spar, as thick as a market lane was wide, had crashed down in the Thieves' Quarter. Even though many joked that a piece of timber that size was the only thing that could have landed in that part of the city without fear of being stolen, the truth was that a couple of dozen people had been crushed to death. It was almost as if it was a reminder that vortexes weren't a trivial matter. What was certain was that they were now a regular part of life in Quentaris.

But this one had been relatively gentle, little more than a rumble coming through Tab's mattress, a couple of minutes of darkness, one or two bricks falling from a wall somewhere nearby, and a sudden pallid brightness which made Tab think of watered-down lightning. It was a relief. A gentler vortex meant less of a clean-up around the farm.

In the street that ran along the other side of the stable wall, Tab could hear excited voices and hurried footsteps. This was as much a part of travelling through a vortex as mixing up mortar for repairing walls. Nor'city Farm was quite close to the edge of the city, and every time Quentaris was taken through into another world, most Quentarans rushed to the edge to look down and see what kind of place they'd been taken to this time.

Quite frankly, Tab couldn't be bothered. She was tired. Besides, she'd find out the next day, when everyone was talking about the colour of the land, whether it was mountainous or flat, dry or lush, populated or deserted. She'd find out, she'd be interested for a moment, and then she'd go back to not caring that much either way.

So for now, unless Bendo barged into her stall and insisted that she clean up some mess or another, she was going to stay right where she was, and she was going to sleep.

6

AMELIA HEARS A STORY

It was an empty world below Quentaris. It had been for days, ever since they arrived through the gentle vortex. Day upon day of endless ocean below, and overcast skies above, with a washed-out sun doing its best to cast its weak glow from beyond the thin cloud.

Tab leaned out over the edge of the parapet and looked down. Beside her, Philmon formed a huge blob of saliva between his lips. It grew and grew, and finally he pursed his lips and let it break free. It fell past the city wall, past the jutting rocks and soil where Quentaris had been torn away from its original site, and continued to pick up speed as it plummeted down towards the blue shimmer of the ocean far below. Then, long before it had even passed the bottom of the 'keel' of Quentaris, it was lost to their view.

'You're disgusting,' Amelia said, but she giggled as a nearby sightseer tutted his disapproval.

'It's not like there's anything down there for it to land on,' Philmon replied. 'It's just a whole lot of

water. Spit plus water equals more water.'

'So, Philmon, what's the word from up in the rigging?' Tab asked. 'It's been fifteen days now ...'

'Eighteen,' Amelia corrected her.

'Is it that many? So, it's been eighteen days since we arrived here, and nothing. No landing parties ...'

'There's nothing to land on,' Philmon said.

'So why are we staying here? Couldn't they call up a new vortex and go somewhere better?'

'I wouldn't know. They don't tell me anything like that. I just work up there,' Philmon replied.

'I wasn't trying to squeeze you for information,' she said.

He smiled. 'Yes you were.'

'All right, I kind of was. But you don't know anything?'

'Not a thing.'

'Maybe we're staying here. Maybe Florian's bored with being a pirate,' Amelia said.

Tab frowned at her. 'Don't,' she said. 'What if someone hears you?'

'I don't care.'

'Well you *should* care. They'll chuck you in Skulum Gate with all the others. And me as well.'

'You should be careful,' Philmon agreed. He turned and looked at the tired sun, which was trying to shine through, and mostly failing. 'I think I'm back on shift soon,' he said. 'It's hard to say with that sun. It doesn't behave like it should. Have you noticed how much shorter the days are?'

'Maybe that's why there's been eighteen of them when I thought there were only fifteen,' Tab mused.

'No, that's because you're bored,' Amelia said. 'Come on, let's go and see how Fontagu's going with the play.'

'Oh, that's not fair!' Philmon wailed. 'I've got to go to work!'

'Well have a great time,' Tab said. 'And see if you can find out anything.'

'I'll do what I can.'

While Philmon slouched off to work, the girls began the ten minute walk to the New Paragon playhouse. 'I still don't know what this stupid play's about,' Amelia said. 'I know nothing about this story.'

'You're such a cultured thing, aren't you?' Tab replied, deciding not to tell Amelia that she'd slept through most of the one production she'd seen. 'You don't know the story of *The Gimlet Eye*?'

Amelia shrugged. 'Should I?'

'Probably.'

'So, tell me about it. And try to make it interesting.'

'Well, it's a bit of an old-fashioned story,' Tab said.

'You mean the language?'

'Not just that. I mean yes, it is written with old-fashioned words, but the story's pretty old as well. You know, with people mistaking girls for boys and boys for girls and snakes for worms and all that kind of carry-on. I can't believe people used to fall for that sort of thing!'

'People haven't always been as smart as they are now,' Amelia said.

'I guess that's true. Anyway, the story goes a bit like this: there's this beastie roaming the mountains near a particular village. All the people who live in the village are getting terrified, because this beast – the Gimlet Eye, it's called – is causing serious havoc. It starts out killing livestock, like horses and mules and sheep and goats and ducks and shickins and all sorts of things.

'So the little ... the commoners put up with this for a while, but eventually they're starting to get fed up with having to lock all their animals away every night. But they're not as fed up with the animals being locked up as the beastie is, and it starts taking unsuspecting people. Anyone alone in the fields, or in the woods, or sleeping rough, the Gimlet Eye takes them.'

'Hang on, why's it called the Gimlet Eye? What does that even mean?'

'A gimlet is a really sharp little tool, kind of like a spike. It's a bit like a very small hand-drill, I think.'

Amelia looked confused. 'And the eye?'

'I'm getting there,' Tab said, with a tiny frustrated shake of her head. 'The Eye kills people by waking them up, or getting their attention, then it takes on the form of a beautiful woman. And when I say beautiful, I mean the most beautiful woman you can imagine.'

Amelia sighed. 'How did I know this was coming?' she said, stepping around a dog that was scratching fleas in the middle of the street. 'There's always a beautiful woman who turns out to be the monster.'

'Not always, but in this case, yes,' Tab said, smiling. 'So the Gimlet Eye takes on the form of a gorgeous woman, and when it's got the attention of the man in question, it holds his attention, and of course he can't move because he's absolutely transfixed by its beauty. And while he's transfixed, it gazes into his eyes, and cooks his brain.'

'Through the eyes?' Amelia asked breathlessly.

'Exactly, through the eyes. And when the victim goes into this state of ... of nothingness, the monster moves in and *ung*! – the man's dead. One bite, there goes the head, chomp chomp chomp.'

'Well, it sounds like a great story so far. A really fun play to take the whole family to.'

'Oh yes, absolutely!' Tab said with a laugh.

A seller from the nearby markets had just slouched by with his high-laden mule. 'Hang on,' Amelia said, 'you just told me that this Gimlet Eye thing turns into a beautiful woman, right? So how does it transfigure –'

'Transfix.'

'Sorry, how does it transfix animals? Does it take the form of an especially lovely lady-goat or lady-donkey?'

'No, I think for the animals it just goes *ung*! To be honest, the original text doesn't really go into its methods of attracting livestock, Amelia.'

'Sorry. I just thought it seemed like quite a major flaw in the story.'

Tab frowned at her. 'And the fact that this

creature can simmer your brains with a stare didn't make you stop and think? Come on, Amelia, these old legends don't care about that kind of thing. You shouldn't get so technical.'

'Very well, but there is one more thing,' Amelia went on. 'If this monster thing likes to turn itself into a gorgeous woman to lure its prey, who are always men, why don't they just send the womenfolk of the village out to kill it?'

Tab stopped walking for a moment and stared at her. 'I don't know, all right? *They just don't!* Should we carry on with the story?'

Amlia shrugged. 'Sure, if you think it's worth it.'

'*Thank* you. So, they decide to hunt this thing down, and there's this one man in the village – a carpenter called Robar, but he's quite poor, and not at all brave. He's also lame, and has to use a stick when he walks, and he barely makes enough money to support himself, his wife and his little dog Fargus.'

'Why doesn't his wife get a job?' Amelia asked.

Tab took a deep breath. 'I don't know, Amelia.

She's got no arms.'

Amelia's eyes were suddenly wide. 'Really? She's got no arms?'

'No! No, of course she has arms – I made that bit up. I don't know why she doesn't work, but she doesn't. And neither does he, really, as I said, because he's lame. And to make matters worse, he's blind in one eye. He's a bit of a mess, truth be told.'

'Sad.'

'It is.'

'Hard, being a carpenter with only ... Sorry. Continue.'

'Thank you. So anyway, when the villagers decide that they're going to hunt down this Gimlet Eye beastie, Robar says he wants to go along.'

'With his walking stick?'

'Exactly. And with his one good eye. And of course everyone in the village thinks that the very idea that he should go along on the hunt is totally hilarious, including his wife.'

'Now *that's* not very kind.'

'Oh, his wife's the worst of the lot! Her name is Sarad, and as well as not helping out with the income, she's a first-rate ... well, let's just say that she's not very nice. And she's always ridiculing Robar, and saying that she wishes she'd married someone brave and strong like Darmas Girth, the local hunter, who thinks that he's the big man in the village. Because the thing is, she's actually quite in love with him.

'Then Darmas Girth leads the hunting party out into the dark woods – without Robar – and they search for days, but can't find the Eye. But one night, when they're about to give up the search, the hunting party is sleeping out in the woods, near a creek of some kind, and Darmas Girth hears the sound of singing, and he wakes up to see a beautiful maiden bathing in the moonlight, singing softly to herself.'

'Oh dear,' Amelia sighed. 'She's naked, isn't she?'

Tab smiled. 'I'm afraid so.'

Amelia chuckled. 'Men,' she said.

'It's a fable, Amelia. So of course Darmas Girth can't look away, he's so captivated by her beauty, and he gets up from his place beside the fire and goes over there, and the beautiful woman turns around and yes, it's the beastie, and it cooks his brain and eats his head.'

'Nice,' said Amelia.

'Isn't it? So all the other men wake up and hear this commotion, and luckily the Gimlet Eye is too busy eating Darmas Girth's head to bother looking like a lovely woman any more, so they see it in all its horrible awfulness.'

'Which is what? What's it look like?'

Tab shrugged. 'I'm not sure. It's just ... horrible.'

'And awful?'

'Yes, very. So the men all run away and go back to the village, and although they're upset that Darmas Girth is dead – but only a bit upset, because even though he was strong and brave, he was also a bit of a bully – they're more disappointed that they haven't been able to kill the Gimlet Eye as they set out to do.'

'Which means they're going to have to keep locking their animals up at night.'

'That's right. But do you know who's most upset about Darmas Girth getting his head eaten? Sarad, Robar's wife. You see, she was secretly in love with him.'

'It wasn't that much of a secret,' Amelia said. 'You told me that just a minute ago.'

'Well anyway, it's a secret to everyone else, including Robar. And when he finds out that his wife is so grief-stricken at the news of Darmas Girth's death, he decides to do something.'

'Let me guess – he decides to go out and hunt the Gimlet Eye himself.'

'Yes! Exactly!' Tab replied. 'How did you know?'

'Just a hunch. But hang on – won't he get his head eaten as well?'

Tab stopped walking and looked at Amelia, a sly smile on her lips. 'He can only fall victim to the Gimlet Eye if he can see it, can't he?'

'I suppose so ...'

'And he's already blind in one eye, isn't he? So do you know what he does?'

'Oh no,' Amelia said, shaking her head. 'He doesn't!'

'He does. He goes out into the woods with his walking stick and his trusty little dog Fargus, and in his pocket he has a small tool from his workshop – a tiny little hand-drill.'

'A gimlet!' said Amelia.

Tab nodded and smiled. 'Exactly. And he hunts for the monster until one night he's sitting by his campfire and he hears Fargus start woofing like mad. The dog's going crazy, and sensing that he's spotted the beastie, Robar takes out the gimlet from his pocket and ...' She paused, watching Amelia for a reaction.

They'd stopped walking, and were in the middle of the street, with people pushing past, walking around them, going about their daily errands. 'What does he do with the gimlet?' Amelia asked, her voice barely more than a whisper.

'I don't know,' Tab replied. 'That's as far as I've read.'

'No!' cried Amelia. 'You must know what happens!'

Tab grinned, and shook her head. 'I'm afraid not,' she said. 'Sorry.'

'You could have said that you didn't know the ending to the story before you started telling it to me!'

Tab shrugged. 'Yes, probably. Oh, look, we're there,' she added, peering up at the front wall and main door to the New Paragon.

The Unja guard at the front door was young and bored, so it was a very simple matter to distract him by 'accidentally' knocking over a water trough in the street, then sneaking into the playhouse while he was watching the ensuing havoc.

The loudest voice the girls could hear as they entered was Fontagu's. 'No, no, *no!*' he was shouting at a poor, hapless young boy in a dress. 'The part of Sarad needs more menace. But not too much. I'm sure you've at least heard of subtlety? She's a complex character, you stupid boy, and you're playing her like some kind of one-dimensional fishwife!' He put his hands to his head and sank back onto a chair, while the boy in the dress and another young man holding an oversized stage sword stood stunned and awkward.

'If only they'd let girls play girls' parts,' Amelia said.

'Or Florian,' Tab replied, and they both laughed.

At the sound of their laughter, Fontagu turned and saw them. 'Friends!' he said. 'Oh, it's so good to see a couple of kind faces. Kind intelligent faces, not like these dolts. Go on, take a break before I see sense and fire you both,' he said to the two actors, who scuttled away backstage.

'Not going so well, then?' Tab asked, leaning on the edge of the stage and looking up at Fontagu.

He groaned. 'If Florian doesn't kill me, the reviews will! It's less than a week until opening night, and look at what I'm working with – wooden swords and a clod in a dress!'

Tab felt something on her foot, and looked down to see a small, fluffy white dog sitting on it. 'Make yourself comfortable, won't you?' she said to it.

'Oh, how cute!' squealed Amelia, bending down to scratch the dog's head. 'Whose is it?'

'I don't rightly know,' Fontagu said. 'It just turned up off the street and took a shine to me. I don't suppose you're an agent, are you?' he asked the dog, before groaning and shaking his head despairingly. 'Then you could get me out of his mess.'

'What's the dog called?' Tab asked.

'I've named him after the dog in the play,' Fontagu said.

'Fargus!' Amelia said proudly. 'Is he going to actually be *in* the play?'

'No, I don't expect so, but I could stick him in a dress and he'd be certain to do a better job than that halfwit you were unfortunate enough to see a moment ago.'

'How are the script changes working out?'

'The ones that Janus made?' Fontagu appeared less than

impressed. 'Imagine the finest thickleberry tart, with clotted cream and a drizzle of lemon whey.'

'Mmm,' the girls said in unison.

'Now imagine a cockroach crawling through it.'

'Ew,' said Tab.

'Uh-uh,' said Amelia.

'Well, the tart is my play, and that horrid insect crawling through it is the page of changes they insisted upon.' Fontagu sighed and stood up. 'Well, you'd best let me get on with it – see if we can't pick around the cockroach. You can stay and watch for a while if you like. Come on, cretins one and all,' he called. 'Dresses on and away we go.' Then he glanced back at the girls and rolled his eyes again.

While Fontagu and the other actors went back to their rehearsals, Tab and Amelia went exploring the New Paragon. The main part of the playhouse was a huge expanse of stone floor scattered with straw, where the audience would stand, looking up at the performers. Around the walls were stalls for those prepared to pay a little more for their tickets, while the royal box was near the side of the stage. The girls sat in the cushioned seats, putting their feet up on the side-tables and looking down their noses at the actors practising on the stage.

'I am Florian the Gross,' Amelia said. 'I am better than everyone here.'

'And I am Janus the Slightly Creepy,' said Tab. 'I have a friend who smells of tigerplums.'

They stayed and watched from the royal box for a while longer, but after seeing Fontagu screaming insults at his poor, bumbling cast for twenty minutes or so, Tab turned to Amelia. 'Torby?'

'Torby.'

Being the middle of the day, they went by the most direct route to the Grendelmire Infirmary, even though that took them straight past the lane that was believed to lead to Skulum Gate.

'Don't even look down there,' Tab said to Amelia as they passed.

'I know it's a bit creepy, but don't you ever wonder —'

'No. No, I don't. If we'd been just a little more experienced, it would have been us, Amelia. We should have been grateful that we were still learning.'

'So why wasn't Stelka sent there?'

'Can you imagine the outcry? No, they needed a reason that people could agree with, so they made up that ridiculous charge and threw her in jail. Come on, don't slow down,' she said, grabbing Amelia's arm and dragging her away from the laneway with the dead end and the cold air.

The Grendelmire Infirmary was three storeys high, with an imposing facade and rows of small, unfriendly looking, barred windows.

'It's sad, visiting Torby here,' Amelia said.

'True, but I think it's important.'

'He doesn't even notice that we're here.'

'I know.'

The room that doubled as an entry hall was empty, so they made their way straight up the stairs to the second floor, where Torby's bed was. He'd been moved from his comfortable space some months before to make room for the dying mother of one of Florian's favoured courtiers, and after she finally died, they'd never bothered to move Torby back. His was the last in a row of a dozen or so beds, which faced another row on the opposite side. About half the beds were occupied, mostly by very old people, and one or two who were muttering madly under their breath.

Torby lay on his left side, his eyes turned to the blank wall. Even when the girls stood at the end of his bed and spoke to him, there was no reaction from him; not even a flicker of the eyes.

'Torby,' said Tab, crouching down beside him and taking his hand. 'It's Tab and Amelia. How are you today? Can you squeeze my hand?'

There was no response. Tab looked at Amelia, and saw tears in her eyes.

'What have they done to you, Torby?' Amelia said.

'It's terrible,' Tab said. 'He's getting so thin.'

'Sorry, but I've got to go,' Amelia suddenly said. Then she turned and half-ran for the door.

'We'll come and see you again tomorrow,' Tab

promised, giving Torby's hand another squeeze. 'Keep hanging on, all right? You'll be fine.'

She headed back downstairs, and found Amelia sitting on the front steps.

'Are you all right?' Tab asked, sitting down beside her.

Amelia wiped her eyes with the back of her hand. 'I hate seeing him like that. He was doing so well, then ... then this.'

'I know,' Tab replied, tucking her friend's hair back behind her ear. 'It's so strange, though. He was getting back into his magic, becoming more confident.'

'There had to be some kind of connection between the Archon dying and Torby going backwards,' said Amelia. 'I bet it had something to do with Florian.'

'You don't know that.'

'True, but don't you think it would be interesting to know what happened to Torby, and whether it was linked? But of course now Torby can't tell us.'

Tab nodded. 'It makes me angry too. But you have to keep your temper under control, Amelia. And you can't just say whatever comes into your head wherever you happen to be. Even if Florian ...' She stopped while a visitor passed them on his way into the infirmary, then lowered her voice a little. 'Even if Florian did make Torby that way, there's no way to prove it.'

'I know.'

'So don't let yourself get so worked up about it.'

'You're right. And what is that disgusting smell?'

'I don't know. I didn't smell it. Oh yes, there it is!'

'That's the smell of tigerplums!'

Tab shuddered. 'Aren't they hideous? There must be a tree around here somewhere.'

'They should cut them all down, if you ask me, the horrid, stinking things.'

THE CAMEO

Fontagu was anxious. It was a matter of days until the opening night of the performance. Already the preparations for Florian's birthday celebrations were in full swing, with a large part of Tarquin's Hill cordoned off for the erection of marquees and stalls for invited guests. The route from the palace to the hill had been inspected several times, and all homeless people, unseemly types or poor folk had been moved elsewhere. The same had been done along the route that led to the New Paragon, where Fontagu was putting the finishing touches to his play.

It was hard work, being the writer, director and star of the show. It was doubly difficult knowing that a dud performance could end up with him ... Well, he didn't like to even contemplate the possibilities – the very thought made him break out in hives. And a leading man with hives would never do.

The changes that Janus had insisted on had been challenging. At first glance, they appeared to be no more than a line here and a word or two there. But then came the big change – a part specially written for Florian himself.

'Lord Janus wants him to feel special,' Kalip Rendana had said weeks before, when he'd dropped in unexpectedly to return the script. 'So he wants him to have a cameo role. A small speaking part.'

'How small a speaking part?' Fontagu asked warily.

'Something near the end. Here, I'll show you where he's made the changes.' Rendana opened the script to one of the later pages and pointed. 'There, where he's marked it.'

Fontagu felt suddenly faint. 'There are lines and lines here. And who is this Calran person?'

'He's an incidental character. Whom the Emperor will be playing.'

Fontagu began to read. '"Greetings, I am Calran, a wandering hawker, out to do no good. I have seen your fine animals and your lovely wife, and wish to take them all for myself, o lame and blind carpenter."'

'Oh, this is terrible!' Fontagu exclaimed. 'What I mean is, this is terribly good,' he quickly added as he saw Rendana's hand go to his belt where he kept his little knife. 'I expect that I might have to tidy up some of the dialogue a little, but ... but I'm a professional, as you know.'

'Of course,' Rendana said, his hand still resting on the pommel of his knife.

Fontagu read on, silently this time. It seemed that after a brief conversation between the hawker and Robar that eventually turned into an argument, a swordfight was to break out, in which Calran was to briefly get the upper hand, but in which ultimately he would suffer a fatal blow.

'Calran's got to look good, but he has to die in the end,' Rendana explained. 'I mean, it's a classic story, or so I'm told, so this Robar chap has to win. But not too easily.'

'I see,' Fontagu said. 'So I get to kill Florian ... Well, Florian's character, I mean,' he added with a nervous laugh.

'That's correct,' Rendana said. 'Lord Janus was anxious to know whether you have one of those stage swords. You know, the ones that look real, but when you push them against something they fold into themselves?'

'Of course,' Fontagu said. 'I've got one right here.' He reached into his personal chest of props and took out his best stage sword, which he waved and flourished about for a moment. 'As you see, good sir, even from very close up, it appears to the naked eye as a genuine sword with which one might do great harm on the body of an opponent,' he said in a loud stage voice. 'But from up close ...' And he lunged forward, taking Rendana completely by surprise, pushing the sword at his abdomen, right to the hilt.

Rendana looked down, his brow furrowed. Then

he began to laugh. 'Oh, yes, I see. That's very good, isn't it? Very realistic.'

'Indeed,' Fontagu replied, somewhat proudly. He withdrew the sword, and the blade returned to its original position. 'See how it appears sharp at the tip, but in fact ...' He ran his thumb over the end. 'Completely harmless.'

'May I?' Rendana took the stage sword from Fontagu and swung it about. Then, with a movement so fast that it had made Fontagu flinch and whimper, he buried it to the hilt in Fontagu's belly. Then he pulled away and swung it around again, grinning like a schoolboy. 'Yes, that should do nicely. Very good. Well, my actor friend, if you can follow the instructions Lord Janus has put in that script, I suspect that all will be well.'

That had been some time ago, and now, with opening night a mere matter of days away, Fontagu's hives were starting to itch.

Were the actors ready? He certainly hoped so. He felt that he himself was ready, and he knew that the play was well written. At least it was well written with the exception of the pointless scene towards the end, where Florian would wander onto the stage, get in a meaningless duel with Robar, and die. Part of Fontagu wished he could use a real sword, but he pushed that thought away. He might have committed some bad deeds over the years, but murder wasn't one of them.

Now, as he stood at the back of the New Paragon playhouse watching the final touches being put on the stage backdrop, he felt a warm tingle in his chest that had nothing to do with hives. He recognised it as the old familiar excitement that he'd not felt for so long. Nerves, but excitement as well.

He felt a warmth on his foot, and looked down. 'Fargus,' he said, bending down and picking up the little dog. 'Are you going to behave on opening night?'

Fargus licked his chin.

'You need to stay backstage and guard all the props,' he said. 'That's going to be your job, my little friend.' He scratched the dog's belly. 'I'm glad you've been around to keep me company. You've been the only other intelligent being in this entire catastrophe. Even without training you could have played the role of the dog better than that knucklehead I've got in the dog suit. Seriously, Fargus, what do they teach in acting school these days?'

* * *

Tab sighed, closed her book and laid it beside her bed. Then she wriggled about, making herself as comfortable as anyone could on a sack stuffed with straw. Opening night of the play was only one sleep away, and she'd finished reading the story just in time.

Oh, the ending! She hadn't seen that coming at all.

The lame carpenter, standing in the woods, hearing his dog going crazy and, knowing that the Gimlet Eye is close, reaching into his beltpouch and taking out his own gimlet. Holding it up as he hears the approaching footsteps of the beast, soft and delicate like a beautiful woman would walk. Seeing the tip of the gimlet sparkling in the moonlight, knowing that to turn around and see the creature would be to doom himself. Turning the point of his gimlet towards himself, directly at his face, and at his one good eye ...

Tab shuddered. It was so horrible, and yet so brave, Robar and Fargus fighting the Gimlet Eye, with the blind carpenter following the sounds of his dog as it hung off the leg of the beast. Then she smiled at the memory of the monster falling, and Robar bringing a lock of its lush, wavy hair back to the village.

And finally, the satisfaction as he presented the lock of hair to his horrified wife, telling her that he'd blinded himself completely because he knew that she'd had eyes only for the hunter, but that he, the carpenter, only had eyes for her. That if he couldn't look into her eyes and see love there, he would rather not see at all.

She sighed again. She really hoped that Fontagu would do the story justice. She felt confident that he would.

* * *

Tab awoke suddenly, breathing hard. Had it been a dream? She couldn't remember dreaming. She'd been awake, thinking about the folk story, and the play, and Fontagu, then she'd been asleep, then ... awake, breathless.

Perhaps there had been something more than the nothing of deep sleep. As she dug down into her mind she remembered something. A scream. It had been a scream so wild and full of terror that even the memory of its existence was enough to make her pull her blanket closer around her shoulders.

She played the tiny fragments of the scream over in her mind, again and again, despite how it made her feel. Was it just a scream? Was it simply a sound forced from a throat in a moment of panic or horror? No, as she replayed it she began to hear a name. *Her* name. >>>Tab! Ta-ab!<<<

She suddenly sat up, straight as the masts that creaked above the city. Her eyes stared into the darkness. 'Stelka!'

In the next stall, Freya made a sleepy moan of protest at the sudden sound of Tab's voice.

'Sorry, Freya,' Tab whispered, her mind racing. How had Stelka called her? Had she found some way to reach back through the mind of the accommodating rat into Tab's head? She had been the Chief Navigator – surely with time and effort a magician as good as she could unravel the strange magic of mind-melding and find her way into Tab's consciousness.

Closing her eyes, she went reaching for the mind of Rat. Just as it usually did, the mind-chatter of others crowded around like voices in an adjoining room, but Rat's was absent. She opened her eyes, shook her head to clear the whispering chatter, and tried again. Nothing. Rat was gone.

It had been such a dreadful scream, and now, as it bounced around in her memory like a blind man in a small room, it continued to horrify her.

She tried once more to access the mind of Rat, squeezing her eyes tightly closed and pushing past the murmurings and distractions. Then it was there. Except this time there was resistance as she squeezed into its mind, as if Rat was unfamiliar with the sensation of an intruding presence.

>>>It's just me<<< she told it.

The mind clamped down around her. It was panicking.

>>>It's just me<<< she said again. >>>I'm looking for my friend<<<

The mind of the rat went suddenly limp, as if the

experience was far too much for it to deal with. It was as if it had fainted from the effort of keeping her out. Then the view through the eyes of the rat appeared, like a candle flame catching onto the wick and beginning to burn properly.

Gently, as if this had never happened before, Tab coaxed Rat forward towards the half-moon of light. >>>I won't hurt you<<< she told it, but there was no reply, not even a shrug.

The rat reached the end of the tunnel and poked its nose out into the light. For a moment Tab was disoriented. The rat in which her mind rode wasn't inside Stelka's cell, but outside, in the corridor, which took her by surprise. Through the bars she could see the crooked table, the low bench that they called a bed, the bucket in the corner, the tipped-over chair. But no Stelka.

>>>Where's Stelka?<<< she asked, and the force with which she asked startled the rat, making it turn and scurry back into its tunnel.

>>>I'm sorry, I didn't mean to frighten you<<< she told it. >>>You're not usually this skittish<<<

Eventually, and with much encouragement, she managed to turn Rat around. Back at the opening of the little tunnel, she gently prodded it forward onto the floor and over to the bars of the cell to have a proper look around.

The instant she screamed, she knew that this rat would never allow her back into its mind. For this rat wasn't *her* rat. It wasn't *the* rat. It wasn't *Rat*. The body of her rat was on the floor near its little triangular tunnel, in a small pool of shiny darkness, with its head lying a good pace or more away. She'd seen it, registered what it meant, and reacted with a scream. And a fraction of a moment later the rat in which her mind was riding had squeezed and panicked and arched, and her mind had been ejected like a drunk from a chapel.

For the second time that night Tab sat on her bed, her eyes wide and her heart pounding. It was only a rat, that was true, but it was a rat which had, with its last thought, provided the passage for Stelka's agonised plea for help as she was dragged off ... where? And it was that which made her pull her cloak around herself, slip on her boots, and begin climbing the wall at the end of the stable. She didn't know how yet, but she was going to find Stelka.

* * *

As she hurried through the deserted streets, Tab considered her options. Verris would have been her first choice, but even thinking about him made her feel terribly, terribly sad, so she quickly pushed the thought away. No point dwelling on things that could never be.

Should she go to Fontagu? No, he was too preoccupied with his precious play. He'd only be dismissive and selfish.

Philmon? Maybe, but most of the time he simply tagged along and did what was needed, but rarely came up with any good ideas of his own. Unless heights were involved, or knots, it wasn't the right time to ask him for help. Besides, he hated being woken up in the middle of the night. He'd stay grumpy about it for hours, maybe even days.

Amelia. It had to be Amelia. She was once a magician as well. Two former magicians teamed up – even very young ones – had to be better than one former magician teamed up with a sky-sailor, a missing former pirate, or a self-obsessed actor.

The other advantage of choosing Amelia was that she was easy to get to. Her room was on the first floor of the Flegis Arms where she now worked, but there was a woodshed and a kind of lean-to at the back of the building that offered fairly easy access to her window ledge. Yes, it was something of a climb, but for someone as agile as Tab, it was about as difficult as climbing a flight of stairs.

She rounded the corner of a building and stopped, stepping lightly into the shadows of an eave. Something felt wrong. She had the distinctly uncomfortable feeling that someone was following her. It felt like something prickling at the base of her neck.

She looked behind her. The street was empty, except for a few barrels and crates stacked outside the door of the building on the opposite side of the narrow street. The windows of the houses and shops around her were all dark – not so much as a glimmer of light from a lamp or a candle. Somewhere far off in the distance a dog barked, and one or two lonely creaks wafted down from the network of rigging overhead. But other than that, nothing.

Tab considered closing her eyes so she could feel around for a mind with which to meld, but to close her eyes and concentrate on searching for a mind would be to lower her guard, and she didn't want to risk it at that moment. Not here, when it was already so dark.

She cleared her throat, and the noise momentarily startled her, it sounded so loud in the silence of the laneway. With another glance over her shoulder, she stepped back onto the pavement, taking care to stay close to the walls.

A moment later she stopped again. She'd heard nothing, and yet she felt so strongly that there was someone very close behind her.

'Hello?' she called, her voice low and timid.

There was no answer, so she continued on. But then, a few seconds later, she felt the urge to stop yet again. 'Hello?' she repeated. 'Is someone there?'

She jumped as a cat snarled nearby. Perhaps that was all it had been – a cat out in the night, off on a mission of its own.

'Come on, Tab,' she muttered, squaring her shoulders and heading up the hill again. It must have been raining while she was asleep, because here and there were small puddles. Some she stepped over, but the larger ones she had to walk around, which took her out into the brighter, more moonlit part of the street. Just as soon as she could, she returned to the shadows.

Again came the awareness that she was being followed, and she stopped once more. But this time the awareness was so strong, almost as strong as a certainty. Crouching down behind a handcart that had been parked near the darkness of a narrow alley, Tab swallowed down the hard-edged lump in her throat and tried to calm her thudding heart. 'There's no one to be afraid of,' she murmured below her breath. 'It's just a cat.'

She wondered if it was time to go searching for a nearby mind again. Perhaps if she began feeling about, she'd find herself in the mind of a cat, she'd see herself crouching in the shadow of the handcart, and then she'd feel better.

Yes, that's what I'll do, she thought. It won't take more than a moment.

She'd just squeezed her eyes shut when she heard a sudden shuffling noise behind her, a little like a ...

VOICES IN SACKS

Tab opened her eyes slowly, and flinched away from the pounding pain in the back of her skull. Everything was dark, and smelly, and stuffy, just as it would be if an old dung sack had been pulled over her head.

She tried to lift her hands, but she couldn't – they were tied behind her.

Oh, well that's just great, she thought wryly. Someone's gone and knocked me over, tied me up and pulled an old sack over my head.

Judging by the rumble and jolting of wheels, the rocking motion, and the clop-clop-clop of hooves, she decided that she must have been in a cart of some kind. She tried to call out, but it was only then that she noticed the rag that had been stuffed into her mouth. The only sound she could make was something between a grunt and a moan.

'Quiet,' a man's voice growled beside her. 'You'll get us all killed.'

By working her mouth back and forth, Tab was finally able to force the rag out. She spat a couple of times to get the musty taste from her tongue. 'Where are we?' she whispered. 'And where are we going?'

'I don't know,' the man said. 'I can't see anything.'

'Have you got something over your head as well?' Tab asked.

'We all do,' replied a third, woman's voice.

'I told you, be quiet,' the man said again. 'We're heading somewhere, and I don't know where, but I'm quite sure we're not going to like it. One thing's for certain, however – it's going to be a lot worse for us if our captors think that we're going to give their game away, whatever *that* might be.'

The man's voice seemed very familiar to Tab, and she frowned to herself as she tried to place it.

'Um ... do I know you?' she asked.

'Are you talking to me?' the man replied.

'Yes.'

'Then it's best you don't. Seriously, you need to be quiet.'

The cart continued rocking along the cobblestones.

'We're heading for starboard,' said the woman's voice. 'We just went past the Quartermaster's Inn.'

'How could you know that?' the man asked gruffly.

'Because the Quartermaster's Inn is the only place that has Fresni folk music on a Bursday evening. Hear that? That's the sound of a grue-harp.'

'You're right,' Tab replied.

'Very good,' the man muttered. 'We're heading starboard. That's one thing we know, at least.'

'Verris?' Tab said, finally managing to place the voice.

'Yes. Why – who's that?'

'It's Tab. Tab Vidler.'

'Tab!'

'This is amazing, Verris! I thought you were dead!'

'Not quite, although sometimes it felt like it. But listen, we *must* keep quiet. I don't know where they're taking us, but I quite suspect that they'd think nothing of killing us. So we need to lie low until we know better what's going on.'

'I can't believe this,' said the woman. 'It all happened so fast. One minute I'm eating my dinner, the next I hear a sound behind me, and I've got a sack over my head. I don't even know why. But what if they're taking us somewhere to kill us?'

'I doubt it. If they'd wanted us dead – and I can't think why anyone would – they'd have killed us by now. No, I think they've got plans for us.'

Plans, thought Tab. She didn't like the sound of that. There was only one way to deal with a plan, and that was to come up with a better one.

'Verris,' she whispered.

Verris grunted.

'We need a plan.'

'For what?'

'To escape.'

She heard him sniff. 'Tab, how can we possibly plan an escape when we don't know where we're being taken, or for what purpose? All we really know is where we are *at this moment*. So sit tight for now.'

'Agreed,' Tab said, suddenly thinking about Philmon. His skill with knots would have been handy.

It was hard to say nothing, so Tab occupied herself trying to mind-meld with the horse pulling the cart. She flicked through the mental noise in her mind like pages in a book, and eventually felt a pressure in her shoulders, a tightness in her thighs, and the cold hardness of a bit in her mouth. She knew she was in the mind of a horse.

>>>I hope you don't mind if I take a look at where we're going<<< she said in her mind, forgetting that the horse might never have been melded with before. In her normal, girl ears, she heard it whinny with alarm.

>>>Sorry<<< she thought, hoping that the horse

might at least have some understanding of apology. Then, so she wouldn't further startle it, she mentally backed away, breathing hard.

After a time – it was impossible to know how long, exactly – the cart began to slow. Then it stopped.

'Steady,' she heard Verris murmur. 'Just do whatever they say, for now.'

The horse stamped and snorted, and the sound echoed about, as if they were in a large room. Tab heard a large, heavy door close. Then the cart jiggled as someone stepped up into it.

'There they are, like I promised,' said a thin, copper-coloured voice.

'Is the pirate here?' asked another voice, thick, like it was speaking through gruel.

'Yes, he's the big one.'

'So that's him, huh? I was starting to wonder if he really existed.'

'Oh yes, he exists all right. They've kept him very safe.'

'And who are these others?'

'That's the interpreter there.'

Suddenly Tab felt her arm being prodded with a foot. 'And who's this?' Thick-voice asked.

'She's the one we've been tailing for a while. The magician.'

'She's pretty small for a magician. So, where'd you find her – Skulum Gate?'

'No, she's young.'

'Right. And who's the runt? What's the boy's skill?'

'Think about it.'

'Oh, right.' Thick-voice laughed. 'Yes, I see now.'

'All right, let's get them unloaded. Big one first, I reckon.'

Any thoughts Tab might have had about resisting disappeared as she felt Verris struggling beside her, and heard a dull, thuddy blow, followed by a grunt.

'What did I tell you about fighting back?' Copper-voice growled.

Then Tab felt hands reaching under her arms and lifting her by the shoulders. 'Just you hold tight there, girly, and nothing bad will happen to you just yet,' Thick-voice murmured in her ear.

Just yet, she thought. *That* sounds reassuring.

She was lowered to the ground, and staggered for a moment in the darkness of her sack. Then she was directed forward with a hand at the nape of her neck. One step at a time, she began to walk tentatively forward. 'Step up,' Thick-voice grunted, and she raised her foot high. The surface on which she stood felt slightly unstable, like she had just walked onto a gangplank. She hesitated. Where were they taking her?

'Keep going, you're not there yet,' Thick-voice said. 'Big step down.'

Tab took one more step, and found herself falling forward. With her arms tied she was unable to break her fall, and crashed heavily onto the floor of wherever it was she'd been led. Behind her, she heard the men laugh, and she fought back the tears that sprang into her eyes. Even with a sack over her head to hide her face, she wouldn't allow herself to cry. She had to keep her wits about her.

Somewhere beside her, she heard a thud, followed by another. Someone was sniffling. Footsteps could be heard around them.

'Barbarians,' she heard Verris say.

'Shut up, pirate,' Thick-voice snapped. 'All right, listen up, all of you – I don't want to have to repeat myself. Pirate, you're in charge.'

'In that case, I order you to let us go,' Verris replied. His voice was cut short by the sound of another thuddy blow.

'Pirate, you're in charge,' Thick-voice repeated. 'You, crying woman, you'll be interpreting.'

'In ... interpreting? Interpreting what?'

Thick-voice ignored her. 'And you ...' – here Tab felt a toe poke her in the ribs – '... you're going to navigate.'

'What?'

'You used to be a magician, didn't you?'

'For a while, but I wasn't much more than an apprentice –'

'Don't worry, you'll do.'

'It'll have to,' said Copper-voice.

'Since I'm the navigator, where exactly am I navigating us to?'

'You'll work it out.'

'I'll work it out? How exactly –?'

Thick-voice cut her off. 'Now listen up, I'm getting tired of all this back-chat. You're on a scout-pod, which you're to crew on a very special mission. We're about to cut you free.'

'You've got to untie us if we're going to do as you ask,' Verris said. 'And mark my words, you'll be dead before you're so much as halfway down that gangway.'

The men laughed. 'You don't think that's been thought of? The ropes that tie you are enchanted. You'll remain bound until your scout-pod is clear of the city, when they'll release. Pirate, you'll find your orders in the mission chest. Oh, and there's a bag aboard with weapons in it.'

'And if we choose not to follow these so-called "orders"?'

'Return prematurely and you'll go back until it's done, as many times as it takes. I'd say it's in your interest to do exactly as you are told, and to do it the first time, wouldn't you?'

'That's all you can tell us?' Tab said.

'You'll not get away with this,' Verris warned.

'Oh, I quite suspect that we will,' Thick-voice said. 'It's all at the pleasure of the Emperor.'

'Shut up!' snarled Copper-voice.

'What? It's all in the orders anyway!'

'Still ...'

'Well, all the best to you. Quentaris thanks you,' said Thick-voice. Then he and Copper-voice both chuckled.

Tab heard their footsteps moving away, and a woody scraping noise. Then, somewhere below them, a loud, echoey grinding sound that made Tab screw up her face in the musty darkness of her sack.

'They're cutting us loose,' Verris said. 'They're taking away the gangway. Try to stop crying – it'll be all right,' he said to the woman. 'What's your name, anyway?'

'Danda,' she replied, her voice quivering. 'I'm sorry that I'm being such a cry-baby, but nothing like this has ever happened to me before. Oo!' she suddenly exclaimed, as the pod shifted slightly beneath them, and began to drop. 'We're moving!'

'Yes, they're sending us groundwards.'

'Groundwards?' said Tab. 'But there *is* no ground. It's just ocean down there!'

'I don't like this,' Danda said.

'Neither do I,' said Verris. 'So, we've got Tab the navigator, and Danda the interpreter, and the boy. You, boy – you're not saying much. What's your name?'

There was no response.

'Maybe he's dead,' Tab suggested. 'He hit the deck pretty hard when they threw him on.'

'Hold on,' Verris said, and Tab felt him wriggling past her. 'He's not dead – I can hear him breathing.'

The scout-pod continued to sink, buffeted and gently tossed in updrafts and air pockets as it descended. Tab closed her eyes under the cover of her sack and stretched her mind in every direction, feeling for anything that had eyes or other senses she could borrow, but there was nothing about. A very slight flicker appeared on the very fringes of her consciousness, but it was gone as quickly as it appeared. Either they were already too far below Quentaris to enable her to reach the minds of anything in the city, or there was something about this pod that was blocking her mind-melding skills.

Then, as she squeezed her eyes shut and probed even further into the blackness, she felt a strange tingling about her wrists. 'My ropes feel like they're getting looser,' she announced.

'Mine too,' Verris replied. 'Just as those thugs said they would.'

'They're much looser now,' Tab said. She began to pull her arms apart behind her, just a little at a time, trying to stretch the loosening ropes. And finally, like unravelling stitching, they fell away.

'They're off!' she said, rubbing her wrists.

'Then get ours off as well – we might be able to do something before we're too far from the city,' Verris said.

Tab pulled the sack from her head. The fresh air hit her face like a bucket of water, and she sucked in huge lungfuls of clean air as she looked around. In the dim light of the moon behind the thin cloud, she could see that the pod was like a small boat, only square, with railings instead of gunwales, and a stubby mast about six feet tall. In one corner was a barrel, in another some ropes were loosely coiled on the deck, a long sack lay against one side, and right in the middle of the pod was a chest, secured to the deck with two heavy metal straps.

'I see the mission chest,' she said.

'Tab, untie me,' Verris said. 'Hurry!'

She crawled over to him and lifted the sack from his head. He blinked and looked around. Dirt or whatever else had been in the sack was caught in his untidy beard, and as soon as Tab had leant behind him and finished loosening his ropes, he wiped his mouth with the back of his hand, and spat.

'That is disgusting!' he said. Then he smiled at Tab and threw his arms around her. 'Tab Vidler! If I had to choose just one person to be on this ridiculous errand with, it would be you.'

'It's been so long, hasn't it?' Tab replied, trying not to wrinkle up her nose at his smell. 'Where have you been?'

'I've been – what's the word? – languishing in one of Florian's dungeons. I hear there was a rumour about me dying of a broken heart.'

'Over a horse,' Tab told him, and he smiled.

'A *horse*? A woman, maybe, but a horse? What is wrong with these people? Come on, let's get the others free.'

While Verris began to untie Danda, Tab went to the small, curled up bundle in the corner. This person wasn't wearing a sack – he was simply wearing a blindfold. As she came closer in the moonlight, Tab began to recognise the face behind the blindfold.

'Torby? Is that you?' she said, even though she knew that it was. His blindfold fell away, and it was indeed Torby, his eyes open, staring blankly into nothingness as he lay on his left side.

Quickly Tab untied his hands, talking to him the whole time. Clearly whomever had kidnapped him didn't know him very well – there was never any need to tie Torby up. He hadn't moved for almost a year, so he was hardly likely to start now!

'Torby,' she said, hugging him close. 'Why are *you* here, of all people?'

'Oh my.' Verris was standing behind Tab, looking down at her and Torby. 'They took *him*? Why?'

'I don't know,' Tab replied.

'He's so ... What's wrong with him? He was doing so well!'

'He got worse just after the Archon died,' Tab explained.

'Didn't we all?' Verris replied. Then he looked up, and Tab followed his gaze. The dark underside of the floating city of Quentaris was now far above them. And below them, in the growing light of the overcast dawn, Tab could see the surface of the ocean.

'Is there any land down there to settle on yet?' she asked hopefully.

Verris walked to the railing and leaned out to look down. 'Nothing but ocean,' he said, narrowing his eyes. 'Nothing but ocean,' he repeated, in a thoughtful murmur. 'I'm trying to remember.'

'Remember what?' asked Danda, who was now standing beside him. She was quite tall, with a long, angular face and straw-like white hair.

'I'm trying to remember which world is all ocean. I can't ... I don't think I've been here before ... or have I?' Verris shook his head again, more firmly this time. He seemed very frustrated with his failing memory. 'I can't remember, but I think it's bad.' He suddenly turned to Danda. 'Apparently you're our interpreter. What language do you speak?'

'I speak several.'

'Care to name them?'

'Um ... well, I do speak Unja.'

'Who doesn't?' Verris replied. 'What else?'

'I also speak Thermali, quite fluently.'

'Hmm, less common, but Thermali speakers aren't exactly rare. Anything else?'

'I know a little Tallis, and I can also speak ... No, that's about it. Yes, that's all.'

'You hesitated,' Verris said, in a tone that, for some reason, chilled Tab's blood. 'What else do you speak?'

'I told you, that's it ...'

'What else do you speak?' Verris insisted, his face suddenly very stern.

Danda's voice was low, as if saying it quietly would make it less likely. 'I also studied Yarka for a time.'

'Yarka.' Verris' voice was just as quiet as Danda's, but he said the word with a tone of dread that almost made Tab's heart stop. 'No one speaks Yarka.'

'Except me,' Danda said. 'It's true.'

'Then that's it. It makes sense, all that ocean. We're going to meet the Yarka.'

Tab took a deep breath. To speak would be to break the moment, to make the feeling of horror that had descended over them feel completely real, rather than some kind of nasty dream. 'What are the Yarka?' she asked at last.

Silence.

'Verris, tell me. Who – or what – are the Yarka?'

'I don't want to alarm you, Tab.'

'It's a little late for that,' she said. 'I'm supposed to be navigating, Verris, so you need to tell me. I deserve to know.'

'Very well,' Verris replied with a sigh. 'Tab, even the Tolrushians are afraid of the Yarka.'

'Oh, I see.'

'No, I don't think you do. Whatever you imagine them to be, they are that much worse.'

'Have you met them before?' Tab asked.

Verris gave a humourless chuckle. '*Met* them? No. I did see a dead one in a jar of alcohol once, but they don't tend to die very much. Perfectly suited to their environment. I'd always hoped I'd never have to meet them face to face.'

'What do they do?'

'Do? Whatever they want.'

'I mean, what do they have that we could want? Or need?'

'The rumour is that they grow icefire, but I don't believe it.'

'Doesn't it make sense?' Danda said.

'You tell us. You've studied the Yarka – what do they do?' Verris asked her.

Danda shook her head. 'I didn't study the Yarka, I just studied their language. I know almost nothing about them. But don't you think it makes sense that they grow icefire? Icefire's what we need more than anything, and they've sent us on this ... ridiculous mission.'

'But why us?' Tab asked. 'There's four of us, and that's including Torby. It's not much of an army.'

'They didn't want to send an army,' Verris said. 'If Quentaris was to assemble an army to fight the Yarka but we didn't win, then we would lose many, many Quentarans for no reason. We can't fight the Yarka, so we need to negotiate.'

'Will that work?' asked Danda.

'The Yarka might be savage, but they're also a proud race,' Verris said. 'They'll hear us out.'

'And if we don't achieve what we have to achieve?'

'Florian will send us again, or someone else.'

'There is no one else,' Danda said. 'There was me, and my tutor, and she died almost a year ago. As far as I know, I'm the only one.'

Verris held her in a long gaze. 'Then you'd better interpret well, hadn't you?'

INTO THE WORLD OF THE YARKA

Torby wasn't speaking. Tab hadn't really expected that he would, but she had wondered if this sudden change in his situation might prompt him into movement, or even vague recognition.

'Torby, I need you to talk to me,' she said.

'It's no good,' Verris said, squinting at the newly risen sun, sickly behind the cloud cover. 'Don't waste your time.'

'It's not wasted time,' Tab replied. 'I'm just trying to get something out of him.'

Verris reached down, took Tab's arm and lifted her to her feet. His eyes were deadly serious. 'I don't mean that talking to friends is a waste of time. I'd like to hear Torby speak just as much as you would. But you need to use your time differently right now. You need to concentrate on this. It was in the chest.' He held out a small notebook. On the front, in fine letters embossed into the leather, was a single word: *ORDERS*. Verris patted it. 'You need to familiarise yourself with these. If you don't, we're never getting back up to Quentaris. Not you, not me, not her, and definitely not Torby.'

Resisting the urge to snatch it from him, Tab took the notebook and sat down to read it.

She read aloud: '*Your mission is simple. Negotiate with the Yarka and attain some of their powerful gems.*

'*Each of you is important to the success of the mission.*

'*Verris is appointed with the task of leading the mission. He has not been chosen for his fighting skills, but for his skills as a leader and a negotiator. He has been kept alive for just this purpose – to fail would be to disappoint Us.*'

'No one will be more disappointed with failure than me,' Verris said.

Tab half-smiled, then went back to reading: '*Your Interpreter is one of the very few Quentarans who can converse with the Yarka. Protect her with the utmost diligence.*

'*Your Navigator will guide you from Quentaris to the Yarka and, with all good luck and care, back again. The ocean is vast, and the Yarka difficult to find. The symbols and magical sayings …*

'They're called incantations, you idiots,' Tab muttered.

'Keep going,' Danda said breathlessly.

'*The symbols and magical sayings contained in the pages that follow will allow Stelka to guide you through the world of the Yarka. She will know how to use them.*'

'Hold on,' said Verris. 'Did you say "Stelka"? So why are you here, Tab?'

'I don't know,' Tab replied. 'I really don't.'

'But can you navigate for us?'

'Of course,' she said, hoping that her false confidence wasn't showing. 'There'll be no problem at all.'

She returned to the orders: '*For Quentaris to achieve what it wishes to achieve, three gems are required.*' Tab whistled. 'Three!'

'I know,' said Verris.

She read on. '*You should bring one gem each back to Quentaris, and your mission will be deemed complete.*'

'But if we bring back one gem each, we'll have one too many,' Danda interrupted.

'Keep reading, Tab,' Verris said.

'*The fourth member of your party shall remain behind as leverage payment. That is all.*' Tab frowned. Lowering her voice so Torby wouldn't hear, she asked Verris, 'So he has to stay behind?'

'So it would seem.'

'As their ... I don't know ... slave? He has to live the rest of his life with these Yarka people?'

'Not exactly,' Verris replied.

'All right, so they're not people, but with these Yarka ... creatures.'

'Not exactly.' Tab saw Verris exchange a quick glance with Danda, who lowered her eyes immediately. 'Negotiations with the Yarka are quite simple, Tab. The chances of success are far greater if you have something to give them in return.'

'That's right. Like I said, a slave.'

Verris shook his head. His eyes were glistening as he levelled his gaze at Tab. 'I'm sorry, Tab, not a slave.'

'Then what?'

'A sacrifice.'

Tab slumped to the floor of the scout-pod. It was as if someone had punched her in the gut, and all the wind had been knocked out of her. 'Are you sure?' she gasped.

'You read it yourself,' Verris answered. 'The fourth member of the party will stay back as payment. And there's only one member of our party who doesn't have an important job to do.'

'I think being a human sacrifice is a pretty important job, don't you?'

Verris smiled grimly. 'You know what I mean, Tab.'

Tab shook her head furiously. 'No. No. It's not going to happen. We're all going back − all four of us.'

'Child, be sensible,' Danda said, reaching out to stroke Tab's hair.

Tab pulled away. 'Don't try to make me feel better! And don't call me Child!'

Danda's voice was annoyingly calm. 'All I'm saying is that if any of us wants to see our families again, we need to follow the instructions in that book there, to the letter. Don't you see?'

'I don't have a family, and neither does Torby,'

Tab retorted. 'Maybe that's why they chose us, do you think?'

'Tab, it's not Danda's fault,' Verris said. 'The orders are very clear. It has to be this way. Torby stays.'

Tab looked over at Torby. He hadn't moved from his position in the corner, curled in on himself like a snail that's been poked with a twig. 'Keep your voice down,' she hissed. 'He might not be saying much, but he can hear every word. Then she went over to him, sank down by his side and stroked his face. 'It's all right, Torby. I won't let them do anything to you,' she said softly.

'Tab,' Verris was saying. 'We're nearly there. Time is short.' He was holding out the book. 'It's time to be the Navigator you were always meant to be.'

'I'll be back,' she whispered to Torby, who showed no response at all.

Tab took the book from Verris and opened it. 'You're in my light,' she snapped.

Just as she expected, the pages were full of symbols and diagrams that would once have meant nothing to her. Even now, out of practice as she was, it took her a moment to get her head around them, but surprisingly quickly the understanding began to return.

'I'm glad you know what you're doing,' Danda said, but she was quickly shushed by Verris.

'So?' he asked Tab.

'Yes, I'm getting it,' she replied. She turned to the copper-bound box and opened the lid. Inside was a small blue velvet bag, and a slightly larger green one. She also saw a humble hinged case, about the size of a child's shoe, and made from a dark, dense wood.

And there, tucked down beside the bags and the wooden case was a rolled-up cloth, a little like a small tapestry rug, which she removed carefully – it was always good to be careful around magic, especially when it had been a while – and laid it out on the deck. She felt a tiny smile growing inside her as she saw more symbols on the tapestry, familiar, like old friends.

She slipped her hand inside the green bag and took out a tiny red claw, like an open hand poised to form a fist. It was mounted on a pedestal carved from aqua-green quartz-like rock. As she placed it on the tapestry she felt the finest feathery tingles passing through her fingers, but rather than feeling frightened by this, she found it to be yet another oddly comforting sensation.

Finally she opened the drawstring of the little bag. A sudden blue glow spilled from its mouth, catching everyone, including Tab, by surprise. She'd known what was in there, and yet she found herself forgetting to breathe as she reached in with trembling fingers and drew out a tiny fragment of icefire, no larger than a grain of rice.

'Don't drop it,' Danda muttered.

'Let the girl work,' Verris said quietly. 'She knows what she's doing.'

Even in the growing daylight, their faces were brightly illuminated as Tab placed the tiny gem into the red claw. With a sound that was felt in the gut rather than heard, the gnarled fingers closed around it.

Tab allowed herself to breathe again. 'Good,' she said. 'Verris, how far are we from the surface now?' she asked as she pored over the pages of symbols and incantations once more.

Verris looked over the edge. 'You've got two minutes, I'd say, maybe three.'

'That should be about right,' she said. 'And it's still just ocean?'

'Just ocean.'

'All right, I need silence,' Tab instructed, throwing a telling glance at Danda. Then, passing her hands over the bright gem, she began to read from the book.

She didn't need words – the symbols were a language all of their own – but they were a language that could never have been written in any other script. They started as something quieter than speech, more like a low guttural growl, and drifted between the growl and wordless, breathy sighs, like the cries of a baby who has lost its voice. Tab had no awareness of how long the incantations went on, but when she reached the end, she sat back on her haunches and

tried to catch her breath. It was as if someone was squeezing her chest.

'Check now,' she said to Verris, who went to the railing of the pod and peered down again.

'What am I looking for?' he asked.

'Um ... it translates to "bowls", whatever that means.'

'Bowls?'

Danda had joined him at the rail. 'Bowls! Yes! There, see?'

Verris was squinting. Then: 'Yes! I see it too! Tab, come and see!'

Tab got to her feet and went to the rail. They were quite close to the surface now, perhaps only three hundred feet or less. And in the odd light the waves of the violet ocean seemed sluggish, as if the liquid was thicker than regular water.

But of greater interest was the indentation just off to one side. It looked like a pothole in the surface of the sea, and was as wide across as the People's Square back in Quentaris. Beyond it was another of these potholes, a little smaller, and when Tab looked harder she saw more. In fact, the closer they came to the surface, the more there were, until they could see that there were hundreds of these depressions, some large, some small, but scattered around the surface of the ocean like pockmarks.

'It seems like we're moving towards that one,' Verris said, pointing at the first crater they'd seen.

'I hope you said your spell properly,' Danda said in a voice that Tab felt quite sure she wasn't meant to hear.

Verris' face was stern as he turned to face Danda. 'It seems to me that your opinion of Tab here has been influenced by her size. But you should know that I've fought alongside this young woman, and I can tell you that she is immensely brave, a very fine person, and an extraordinary magician. Furthermore, once the time comes for you to start interpreting, she isn't going to be standing next to you saying, "Are you sure you said that word properly?" I trust I'm being clear.'

'Very well,' said Danda, tilting her nose slightly

upward. 'I can see that my opinion isn't welcome.'

'Your opinion is welcome, but in this instance, unnecessary.'

Tab felt a tiny smile growing, deep in her chest. She hadn't realised just how much she'd missed Verris and his forthright, passionate manner.

They were approaching the depression in the ocean's surface rather more quickly now, almost as if some invisible force was drawing them in, faster and faster. And it was only then that Tab thought to feel afraid. Up until that moment she'd been busy, making sure that her spell was uttered correctly, worrying about whether or not she'd get it done before they landed, trying not to let Danda annoy her, and being

concerned about Torby. But now, with the distance between them and the silent, slow-moving waves closing, she finally allowed herself to think about what they might find. Or if in fact they might find nothing, because there was absolutely no sign of life to be seen at all. Except for the depressions pocking the ocean, it was as desolate and endless as anything she could ever imagine.

'Ten feet,' Verris said. 'I think we should probably find something to hang onto.'

While Verris and Danda dropped to the deck and clung to the railing supports, Tab slid across the boards to Torby and threw herself over him. 'It'll be all right,' she whispered. 'I promise.'

But even as she said it, she knew that she was making a promise that she might never be able to keep.

* * *

It was over so quickly. One minute Tab was holding Torby tightly, her eyes squeezed shut, and the next ... silence. Complete silence.

She opened her eyes and looked around. The light had changed. Above the surface of the ocean it had been morning, just on dawn, but down here the pearly light was somehow brighter. Its luminescent blueness reminded her of opening her eyes underwater on a bright summer day, back when there was time for swimming. Back when there was summer and fun, rather than the constant vortexes in the sky and strange lands below.

Overhead, the sky was low and glassy, and moved slowly in waves.

On the other side of the pod, Verris and Danda had sat up and were looking around as well.

Verris spoke first. His voice sounded muffled and distant. 'Everyone all right?' he asked.

'Fine,' Danda replied, her voice also dull and muted.

'Tab?'

'I'm fine,' Tab answered. Her own voice filled her head, as if she had her fingers pressed into her ears. She checked on Torby. There had been no change. His eyes were open, he was breathing, but other than that, he was like the shell of a person.

She stood up, and felt herself being held back by a surrounding pressure. Then, as she turned, she found her feet coming off the deck slighty. Instinctively, she waved her arms up and down, and her feet lifted even higher. It was like she was flying. Flying slowly through thick, heavy air. But then she sank back down onto the deck.

'Um ... this is just a thought,' she said, 'but are we ... underwater?'

Verris looked up at the low, silver-blue sky, rippling above. Then he too began to flap his arms, and was soon drifting around above the deck. 'You know, I believe we are,' he said at last, a half-smile on his

face. 'This is indeed strange magic. Underwater, but talking and breathing.'

'And not floating away, either.'

'I don't like it,' said Danda.

Ignoring her, Verris went to the railing and looked over the side, and Tab half-walked, half swam over to join him. Below the pod was nothing but deep blue-green, blending into the most impossible blackness.

'Oh my,' Tab breathed. 'That's deep.'

'Indeed it is.'

'So, Verris, you're the expedition leader,' she said. 'What happens now?'

'You're the appointed navigator – you tell me.'

'Um ...'

'The book, Tab.'

'Oh, of course.' She went back to the little copper-bound chest, with the icefire fragment beside it on its mat, still glowing coolly in its red fist. She opened the book, and the pages swayed slightly in the water.

'Anything?' Verris asked.

'Yes, there's something here,' Tab said. 'Should I do it now?'

'You're the navigator.'

Again, Tab began to 'say' the incantation, with its guttural yet high-pitched wordlessness. Almost imperceptibly the pod began to move again, sinking lower in the water, like a body drifting towards the ocean floor. The pressure was beginning to build, and yet at no time did Tab think to worry. Her confidence was returning, and she took comfort in the symbols and diagrams before her.

Unless they were being sent into a trap ... She pushed that thought away. Now was not the time to be panicking. It was certainly no time to be sending Danda into a panic, and judging by the look on her face, she wasn't far away.

'You're doing well,' Verris said, and Tab smiled at him, to thank him. He seemed very calm, which Tab found comforting. They'd been through a lot together, and she trusted him much more than anyone should ever trust a one-time pirate. She also knew that if at any point he should start looking concerned, that would be a perfect time to start panicking.

'There's some kind of light,' Danda said from the railing, and Tab and Verris went to see. It was difficult to tell how far away the spot of light was, but it was definitely there, if a little blurry. And they were moving towards it.

'Excuse me for a moment,' Verris said, stepping over to the long sack in the corner. From it he drew a sword, long and curved. He snorted as he held it up. 'That's it? A Babdhir sabre? If I'd known that was what they were going to give me, I'd have brought my own. I collected a number of these back when we fought those maniacs, just as mementos. They do have a tendency to break, though.'

'The sabres, or the Babdhir?' Tab asked.

'Both.'

'Is there anything in that sack for the rest of us?' Danda asked.

Verris looked at her levelly. 'Ever used a sword, Danda?'

She shook her head.

'Then I wouldn't let you use one anyway. You'll just cut yourself, or even worse, me. Everyone should do the job they've been sent here to do – I do the leading and any fighting that needs to be done, Tab does the magic, Danda does the interpreting and ...' He stopped, and Tab saw his eyes flicker towards Torby. 'So,' he ended, removing the sabre from its scabbard and swinging it about. It moved listlessly through the water.

'Hey, that's going to be pretty effective,' Tab said. 'Swoosh, swoosh, swoosh.'

'Old habits,' Verris said, returning the sabre to its scabbard and dropping it on the deck with a muffled clang. 'It's probably better we don't show up armed to the teeth anyway.'

The light was much closer now, and Tab could see that it came from a round door or window or some other opening of some kind, set into a huge dark orb, which was darker even than the blackness of the ocean depths beyond it.

'I wish I could steer this thing,' Tab said. 'I'd turn us around and high-tail it out of here.'

'Steady,' Verris said as the pod neared the orb. It was looming now, enormous, and somehow in the cold light reflecting from the sides of the pod, she could see that its surface was smooth, like glass. And clean. Not a barnacle, not a scratch.

'I think we've found the Yarka,' Tab said. 'Or at least, we've found where they live.'

They were no more than ten feet from the orb when the pod came to a complete stop. The opening was several feet across, and the glow coming from it, while bright, didn't make Tab feel like squinting or blinking. It was as if the light, like everything else, was struggling to make its way through the heavy water.

'So, what happens now?' Danda said. The water muddied her voice, but it couldn't disguise its waver.

'Shh.' Verris raised his hand and turned slowly on the spot, his long hair trailing behind and around him. 'Now we wait.'

Even time was sluggish down here, and as Tab gazed into the light from the orb she found her mind drifting. It felt most peculiar. Here she was, below the surface of a strange ocean, breathing water like a fish, hovering in a rudderless vessel so far down into the depths that light was soaked up by the darkness. And the portal in the side of the glassy orb continued to glow, staring at her, while she stared back.

She was suddenly brought back by the sound of Danda's voice. 'Is this the only one?' she said. 'Is it just us and ... this?'

Then, as if they were awakened by her question,

other lights began to show. Their appearance was sudden, not like lighting a lamp or a candle, where the wick must catch, then build to a flickering warmth, but immediate. The same cold bluish light appeared in a spot to their right, then to their left, then below, above, everywhere, one after another. And as each light reached them through the water, the orb from which it came showed up as well, dark and alien. There were tens ... no, hundreds, perhaps even thousands of the dark structures, hovering in the water all around, each of them with its glowing round window pointed directly at them.

'I think what you meant to say was "Is it just us and *these*?",' Verris said solemnly. 'And yes, that's exactly what it is – *just* us and ... these.'

GOATS AND FLYING BRICKS

Amelia was feeling ill. Worrying could do that, and the person she was worrying about was Tab.

She hadn't been concerned until she arrived at Nor'west City Farm to find that Tab wasn't there. Bendo was, though, looking furious. 'Where is that friend of yours?' he demanded. 'She's in trouble, I tell you.'

Amelia shrugged. 'I haven't seen her all day,' she replied. 'I was hoping you might know where she was.'

'Well I don't,' he snapped. 'So if you do come across her, you should warn her that when I see her there'll be hell to pay.'

'I'll be sure to let her know,' Amelia replied.

Philmon was on a day off. She found him outside his quarters, sitting against a wall in the dim overcast daylight. He was reading a book, and seemed a little annoyed that Amelia would interrupt his day off to ask if he'd seen Tab.

He laid his book in his lap and sighed. 'Amelia,

what you're forgetting is that I don't keep an eye on every single movement Tab makes,' he said. 'You know what she's like – she's always off on one kind of adventure or another.'

'I guess that's what's worrying me,' Amelia said. 'Most of the time when she gets into these adventures she's got you or me to look after her.'

'I don't think she needs all that much looking after,' Philmon said. 'Most of the time it's her looking after us. You know, I think she'll probably turn up at any moment with a cheeky grin on her face.'

Amelia tried to smile. 'You're right, Philmon. I should stop worrying.'

Philmon picked up his book again, and Amelia turned to leave. Then she stopped and faced him again.

'Can I ask you something?'

Philmon returned his book to his lap and looked up. 'What is it?'

'How long since you've seen Torby?'

'I don't know – a few days. Why?'

'I just got a feeling that I should check on him.'

Philmon scratched his ear. 'A feeling?'

'Yes. It wasn't a big feeling, more just a ... a thought, I guess.'

'About Torby?'

'Yes. Do you think that's weird?'

Philmon shook his head. 'I think about people all the time, but it doesn't make me wonder if it's weird.'

'I know that. I just ... It's a very icky feeling, Philmon, right here.' She rested her hand on her stomach.

'You've probably eaten a bad thickleberry tart.'

'We both know there's no such thing as a bad thickleberry tart. No, it's strange, I know, but I really feel that I need to go and see him. Will you come with me?'

Philmon sighed and closed his book. 'It doesn't look like I'm going to get this finished today.'

'What's it about?' Amelia asked.

'It's a retelling of *The Gimlet Eye*. It's not the full-length version, though. It's one of those condensed book thingies. But I thought I should read it before we go to see the play. It's not a bad yarn, actually.'

'Excellent. You can explain it to me on the way.'

The nursemaid in the entry hall of the infirmary was busy. Or at least, she gave a very good impersonation of someone who was busy. She tutted and sighed, and continued writing in her large book. 'I really don't have time for this,' she complained. 'You'll just have to wait.'

'Look, it's very simple,' said Philmon. 'We just want to see our friend. We come in here quite often, and it's never been a problem before. Can't we just go up?'

'You do know that I'm a magician, don't you?' Amelia said.

The nursemaid glanced up at her, a sneer on her

lips. 'I know who you are, and I know you used to be a magician. Or it was in fact an *apprentice* magician, wasn't it? Otherwise ...' She finished the sentence by mouthing the words 'Skulum Gate'.

'Yes, that's true,' Amelia muttered. 'But I still learnt some pretty good spells.'

'Don't threaten me,' the nursemaid replied. 'I'll get to you when I'm good and ready.' Then, almost as if to emphasise the point, she bit on her thumbnail while she took a moment to read back over what she'd just written. Finally, after she'd written no more than a couple of words to finish, she laid the pen down and looked at them. 'Now, children, can I help you?'

'We'd like to see our friend Torby,' Philmon said.

The expression that crossed the nursemaid's face sent a sudden shudder through Amelia, not quite as strong as the bad feeling that had sent her to Philmon to begin with, but still an unpleasant sensation that crawled across the back of her shoulders.

The nursemaid's eyes narrowed, and her voicebox bobbed as she swallowed suddenly. 'Torby, did you say?'

Philmon nodded, 'Yes, Torby. You know, the boy who lies there with the blank face.'

'Oh, I know who Torby is,' the nursemaid replied. 'But you want to see him?'

'Yes please.'

'Just to see if he's all right,' Amelia added.

'I see. Could you give me just a moment?' the nursemaid replied, standing up in such a hurry that she almost knocked her chair over. 'Excuse ... excuse me.' And she left the room, her skirts swishing around as she bustled out and headed down the long, echoey corridor.

'What do you think that was all about?' Amelia asked Philmon.

He shook his head and shrugged. 'I don't know.'

At the far end of the corridor, the nursemaid was talking to another, smaller woman, with a stern, officious face. Amelia recognised this second woman as the head of the place. She'd seen her around the infirmary, but they'd never spoken.

The conversation between the two women drew

to an end, and the head of the infirmary nodded curtly, before striding officiously towards Amelia and Philmon.

'I've got a bad feeling about this,' Philmon said quietly.

'Have you got it too?' Amelia asked, her hand going to her stomach.

'I don't mean that kind of bad feeling. It's not all magicky or anything. I just feel like she's bringing bad news about Torby.'

Amelia's mouth was dry as she said, 'I think you might be right. I hope you're wrong, but I do think you might be right.'

The head of the infirmary came into the room, with the nursemaid following a short but respectful distance behind. 'Good morning. I'm Myla – I'm in charge here.'

'We've seen you before,' Amelia said.

'Now, you're looking for your friend?'

'Yes, Torby. But we know where his bed is. There's no need for all this fuss ...' Amelia began to say.

Myla gave a very quick, flickering smile, but her eyes remained very serious. 'You might know where his bed is, but do you know where he is?'

'I beg your pardon?' asked Philmon.

'He's not here.'

'So where is he?' Amelia asked.

Myla shook her head. The flickering, humourless smile was back again for a moment. 'He's gone.'

'Gone?' Philmon said. 'Gone where, exactly?'

'We don't know – he just disappeared,' the nursemaid interjected. 'Oh,' she added quickly as Myla cast her a withering glare.

'She's right,' Myla said. 'He disappeared some time last evening.'

'Wasn't anyone watching him?' Philmon asked, his face beginning to redden. 'I mean, he doesn't even move!'

'We were otherwise occupied,' Myla explained.

'Yes. Things were falling down on the goat, you see,' the nursemaid explained. 'Plus there was the –'

'Risha!' Myla turned her head slightly to one side and cut the nursemaid off mid-sentence. 'That will *do*. There are patients who need seeing to. Now,' she added firmly as the nursemaid opened her mouth to argue.

She watched Risha leave, before returning her attention to Amelia and Philmon. 'Last night, a wall fell down in the rear courtyard.'

Philmon frowned. 'A wall?'

'That's right. Plop. Went right over.'

'And what does that have to do with Torby?'

'Or a goat?' Amelia added.

'This is a little embarrassing, but we – by that I mean me and the three other women who work here under very trying and difficult conditions, I might add – were out in the courtyard trying to put out the fire and free the goat.'

'Free the goat?' said Philmon, shaking his head slowly. 'This is unbelievable! If it wasn't so serious it'd be funny!'

'I don't understand,' Amelia said. 'So you were outside trying to free the goat from what? Did the wall fall on the goat?'

'Yes, that's what I'm trying to tell you,' Myla said. 'The goat was tied up to the lemon tree, right beside the wall. And then, somehow, the wall came down on the goat. It also flattened part of our kitchen, and started a small fire. The cook's had to take the day off, he was so shaken by the incident.'

'This is terrible,' Amelia said.

'Oh, it's all right – the goat's fine. Her milk might be a bit off for a couple of days, but that's probably all. But as for our –'

'We don't care about the stupid goat!' Philmon snapped, and Myla blinked in surprise. 'What's upsetting me is that while you and your staff were out the back pulling some farmyard animal out of a pile of rocks, *our friend was being kidnapped*!'

Myla cleared her throat. 'Let's not get ahead of ourselves. We don't know that he's been kidnapped –'

'Well let's see: is he in his bed? No. Is he sitting *beside* his bed? No. Is he anywhere in this building? I assume you've looked for him?'

'Of course. And you're quite right, he's not here.'

Amelia thought Philmon's head was going to burst

with rage. 'Look, if someone who hasn't spoken or moved for almost a year suddenly leaves their bed and disappears, I'd say there's a good chance that they've been kidnapped, wouldn't you?'

>>>Armla! Armla!<<<

'Ah!' yelped Amelia, as a sudden pain ripped through the space behind her eyes. Her hands went to her forehead, but no matter how hard she pushed, the pain wouldn't stop.

And there was the voice, like the sound of grinding teeth. >>>Armla! Armla! These is steel kelp!<<<

'Amelia, are you all right?' Philmon asked, placing a steadying arm around her shoulders.

'Do I look all right?' she said through clenched teeth. 'Something's happening. Someone's trying to say something to me.'

'Are you sure?' asked Myla.

'No, I'm creating a diversion. Of course I'm sure!'

'No, well you don't look at all well. There is a bed just through here. Come this way. Risha! Risha!' she called.

But as quickly as it had come, the pain went, along with the teeth-grinding voice. Amelia felt suddenly drained, her energy depleted, and stumbling forward to a nearby stool, she sat down carefully.

'What was it?' Philmon asked.

'I'm fine,' Amelia replied. This wasn't what Philmon had been asking – she knew that – but she didn't want to talk to him about it until they were alone. Myla and the nursemaid, who was now fussing around getting a cup of water for Amelia, didn't need to hear what she was about to tell Philmon.

She was going to tell him that someone had been trying to mind-meld with her, but that she didn't have a clue who it was.

* * *

'So tell me again, what did the voice say? Tell me exactly.' Philmon seemed excited at this new development. Excited and thoughtful.

Amelia glanced around to make sure that no one could hear her. There was no chance of anyone within the infirmary overhearing her, since the door had been shut rather firmly behind them when they left. But these days it was hard to know who to trust out in the street.

'Come over here,' she said, leading Philmon to one side, near the path that led around to the back of the infirmary. 'I told you, the voice sounded as if it was saying something like "Armla, armla, these is steel kelp".'

Philmon screwed up his face as he thought about this. 'That's strange,' he said at last.

'I know. I've been going over it in my mind, and I think it might have been meant to sound like "Amelia, Amelia, this is steel kelp", whatever *that* means. Steel kelp ... Steel –'

'No!' Philmon said suddenly. 'No, I've got it! It's saying "Amelia, Amelia, this is Stelka". Help. Could that have been it?'

'Of course!'

'So why wasn't she clearer?'

'The thing about the mind-melding is that Stelka's not very good at it yet. I mean, Tab's been teaching her through the mind of a rat, for goodness sake.'

'And can you do it? Can you mind-meld?'

'Tab's tried to teach me, but it's not a skill you can just pick up, like playing hooey.'

'I know that, but I didn't ask if it was hard. I asked you, can you do it?'

'I've managed once or twice, but it's hard to get right. I've watched Tab do it – she's amazing.'

'Yes, well in case you hadn't noticed, Tab's not here, so it's up to you. Did Stelka give you any kind of hint of where she might be?'

'No, she only said what I told you.' Amelia frowned. 'This is getting very strange now, Philmon. First Tab disappears, then Torby, and finally Stelka sends a message asking for help.'

'You said "finally". There's no guarantee that there's anything final about it. For all we know, we could be next.'

'Don't,' Amelia replied. 'That's not funny.'

'Do you see me laughing?'

'So, what now?'

Philmon scratched his ear. 'Do the goat, the falling

wall and the fire strike you as a little odd? Especially considering that while all that was going on, Torby disappeared.'

'Connected?' Amelia said.

'What do you think? Since we have no other leads just now, we should probably check out this wall and the burnt-down kitchen. Do you know where it is?'

'She said it was around the back. Come on.'

Trying to ignore the dull headache that lingered after the message from Stelka, Amelia led the way around the back of the infirmary. The gate in the little archway was locked firm. Philmon jiggled the latch, then craned his neck to peek over the gate. He glanced up at the wall, which was far too high to climb over, then went back to jiggling the gate.

'No, it's no good. We'll go around the other side,' he said at last. 'There's a laneway that runs along the other side of the wall.'

'Can you see where's it's fallen over?'

'Yes. It's a bit of a mess.'

They hurried around to the other side, and down the narrow lane that ran along the starboard side of the infirmary. The lane was empty, and the courtyard wall was slumped over in the middle. Several rows of bricks had fallen in, and were now rubble on the courtyard paving stones.

'Oh, that poor goat!' Amelia said. 'I'll be surprised if it ever gives milk again!'

She stepped closer to the gap in the collapsed wall

and looked across at the kitchen. A small added-on section jutted out into the courtyard, and part of its corner had been struck by some of the falling bricks. The damage from the bricks was minor, but not so the damage from the fire. Above the broken window, the eaves had been blackened by smoke, and the smell of fire and damp ash hung in the air.

'How do you think that happened?' she asked.

Philmon shrugged. 'I don't know – there are dozens of ways a fire can start. A brick fell through the window and knocked something into the stove, maybe?'

'Must have been a pretty light brick, or a brick with wings,' Amelia said. 'Look where the chimney comes through the roof.'

'And?'

'The stove's way over on the other side of the kitchen. That fire didn't start by accident. This was a diversion.'

'Hmm,' Philmon said. He was busy inspecting the part of the wall that was still standing. 'This is interesting.' He pointed at a mark about halfway up the bricks. 'What does that look like to you?'

'Um ... mud?'

'Look down here,' he said, pointing at the base of the wall.

Amelia looked down at a large patch of mud. There were footprints in it.

'So?'

'Someone's tried to climb this wall. See how they've stepped in the mud, then tried to climb over and left mud smeared on the bricks? And their weight on the wall has made it fall down.'

'Yes, onto a defenceless goat,' Amelia said. 'Poor thing.'

'Hey, hold up, what's this?' Philmon said, bending over and picking something up. It was small, about the size of a peanut. 'What do you make of this?'

Amelia shook her head. 'I don't underst ... It's a pip, Philmon.'

'I know. And there's another one here.'

Amelia was beginning to think that her friend might have finally lost it. 'I don't know why that's such a huge discovery,' she said.

'Do you know what kind of pip it is?'

She took it from his fingers and looked at it closely. Then she sniffed it, and screwed up her nose. 'Yes, of course I do. It's a tigerplum pip. And now my fingers will be stinky for a week.'

'Exactly – a tigerplum pip.' He was already turning to go. 'And do you know what that means? It means we know who kidnapped Torby.'

'You can't prove it!' Amelia said as she jogged after him. She was getting the unnerving feeling that he was going to turn left at the end of the lane and make for the palace to have words with Kalip Rendana.

'Amelia, when all the evidence points to one person, that's who you have to talk to first,' he was saying.

'But that's what I mean! The evidence *doesn't* all point to Rendana. Let's look logically at what we know: he took Fontagu's script, which he returned, by the way; we know he works for Janus, who works for Florian, who is a rotter. And we know Rendana has a little knife that he uses to scare people.'

'Exactly!' said Philmon.

'But none of that proves that he pushed down a wall, almost killed a goat and set fire to an infirmary kitchen just so he could kidnap someone. That could have been anyone!'

Philmon stopped. 'You're right,' he said. 'You say that all of that doesn't prove a thing, and I was starting to believe you. But then you mentioned his little knife. Follow me.'

He ran to the end of the lane, but instead of turning left towards the palace, he turned right. Amelia raced after him, following him along the street in front of the infirmary, and back to the locked gate that led into the courtyard from the other side.

'There,' he said, grinning and running his fingers over the edge of the gate. 'Now do you believe me?'

'What am I meant to be looking at?'

'*There!*' He pointed at a collection of fresh scars and scratches in the timber of the gate, just near the latch. 'Do they look like the kind of marks someone would make trying to get through a locked gate? The kind of marks they might make with a little knife?'

'Very well, I admit it,' Amelia agreed. 'But I still don't think you should march up to the ... Oh no,' she sighed. 'Where are you going, Philmon?'

Calling back over his shoulder, he said, 'To the palace. I'm going to have words with Rendana.'

Amelia caught up with him just as he reached the street. She grabbed him by the arm and spun him around. 'Philmon, think about this for a minute.'

'What is there to think about? We need to ask this man where he's taken our friend.'

'What, and you think he's just going to tell you? You think you can just walk up to him and say, "Hello, I'm Philmon, and this is Amelia, and we want to know where our ... Oh, look, I've got a *little knife stuck in my gut!*"? Come on, Philmon, not only does he work for Janus, but there's a whole squad of huge, ugly Unja guards out the front of that palace. Now I think about it, you won't have to worry about getting a knife stuck in your gut, because you're going to get speared to death by Unja soldiers before you even get through the gate.'

Philmon closed his eyes and heaved a deep breath. 'You're right,' he said, his shoulders slumping forward. 'You're right. I just want to know where Torby is. And Tab. And Stelka.'

'Yes, and so do I. And I've just had a better idea.'

A NEW PLAN

'It'll never work,' Fontagu said, nervously glancing around the New Paragon's backstage area.

'Can't we at least try?' Amelia pleaded.

Fontagu shook his head. 'It's foolish. And we shouldn't be discussing it here.'

'We're alone,' she said.

'You can't be sure. You can't ever be sure any more. And your plan won't work.'

'Are you doubting yourself?' Philmon asked.

Fontagu scowled at him. 'Whatever could you mean by that?'

'You say that getting into Skulum Gate can't be done. Is that because you don't think you can prepare a disguise that's good enough?'

'Now let's not go too far,' Fontagu warned. 'I've been working in the theatrical arts for –'

'It's true, though, isn't it?'

'Look, it's not all that important,' Amelia told him. 'We just need to see someone.'

'But in Skulum Gate? Why there, of all places?'

'I need to see someone who lives in there,' Amelia explained. 'It's important, Fontagu. We wouldn't ask if it wasn't. We have to find our friends. Your friends.'

'Oh, wait!' Fontagu clapped his hands twice, threw open a wardrobe chest and began pulling clothes out of it. 'I could do you a lovely palace guard's outfit – you could wander in there and ask Florian anything you wanted!'

'She doesn't need to get into the palace,' Philmon said. 'She needs to go to Skulum Gate.'

Fontagu began to wring his hands together. The knuckles of his long fingers popped and crackled. 'Please, children, I beg you, don't go down there. It's a bad place! It's very bad. It's where all the dregs live now, all the magicians that fled when Florian took over.'

'Yes, and many of those "dregs" are my old friends. And so we're clear, they didn't flee – they were sent there.' Amelia could feel her face beginning to flush red and hot. 'They were supposed to feel grateful that they weren't tossed over the side like some. And they're not bad people – not if you know them. If you think they are, you've been spending far too much time with Florian and his horrid little friends –'

'Shh,' said Philmon, placing his hand on Amelia's shoulder. 'Calm down.'

'Oh, it just makes me cross,' she said. 'It makes me cross that I have to get a disguise to go to talk to my old friends.'

'Why do you need a disguise to go to Skulum Gate anyway?' Fontagu asked.

'Just in case Florian has people watching the entrance,' Philmon said. 'Amelia needs a disguise that she can throw away as soon as she comes out. We'll pay you for it.'

'It's a bad idea,' said Fontagu. 'Besides, how can I concentrate on opening night if I know you're in danger? And knowing that I've been an accessory to —'

'Can you help us or not?' Amelia asked him. 'Because if you can't ...'

'Very well, very well. But if you get caught, I'll deny that I was ever involved.'

'I wouldn't expect anything else,' Philmon muttered.

* * *

'I just noticed something, old woman,' Philmon said as he and Amelia took one of the back lanes leading towards Skulum Gate.

'Oh yes? What is it?'

'You know how Fontagu said that if we got caught he'd deny everything?'

'Yes.'

'His name is stitched inside the neck of that cloak you're wearing.'

Amelia laughed. 'That's funny.'

'Not as funny as you,' Philmon said. 'He's actually

done a pretty good job, you know. I keep looking at you and wondering who it is I'm walking along with.'

'Yes, well you're not walking along with anyone any more. It's time to make yourself scarce. We can't have anyone seeing you with the old woman who's about to go into Skulum Gate.'

'Are you scared?' he asked.

'A little. To be honest, I'm more scared of getting caught when I come out. But I bet I'm not as scared as Torby was when he was taken.' She shuddered then, as she remembered Stelka's voice, screaming out in her mind. 'And I know I'm not as scared as Stelka.'

'Well, all the best. I'll be waiting right over there,'

Philmon said, pointing to a small flight of stone steps that led up to another, higher street. 'I'll see you soon.'

'With any luck,' she replied.

It was hot under the wig and all the make-up, even with the weakness of the sun's rays through the cloud cover. Amelia bent over a little more, reminding herself of the last thing Fontagu had said: 'Less is more'. He'd told her how the best actors didn't overact, but rather sank into the role in a natural way. She'd almost laughed when he told her that, since she'd always thought that Fontagu's whole life involved overacting.

'You might smile, sweet one, but nothing will get you noticed faster than trying not to get noticed,' he'd said.

But it was good advice nonetheless, and the closer to Skulum Gate she got, the more she had to remind herself that she wasn't a young former apprentice magician on a mission, but an old woman out walking the street.

The temperature fell noticeably as she rounded the last corner and stepped into the lane which led to Skulum Gate. She took a deep, fluttery breath. At the end of the street was ... nothing. A dead end. The wall of a double-storey building stood there, leaning slightly inward. Its windows were empty. Dead.

'Calm, Amelia,' she muttered as she stepped forward. The further in she went, the cooler it seemed to get, and the drier her mouth became. As well as that, the walls on either side were closing in. With a struggle, she resisted the urge to look back. She'd really thought that going into Skulum Gate during the day would be the easy option, but now that she was approaching the entrance, it felt anything but easy.

She was almost at the very end of the alleyway now, and was just beginning to think that she'd come into the wrong lane when a deep chill passed over her. She shuddered all over. She was sweating, and yet she felt terribly, terribly cold, as if she had a fever.

Somewhere behind her eyes she felt noise, conversations, cries and moans. Her fingers tingled and her toes began to cramp. And that deep thrumming pain in her stomach was back, but it wasn't nerves. It was something of a far more magical nature, and not necessarily the good kind.

Skulum Gate proper was immediately to her right. It was a small, rather unimpressive archway, cleverly hidden from view until she'd been right upon it. The archway was free-standing, and looked to lead into an open courtyard, and yet the light through the gap was darker in some way. Was it like a shadow? No, it seemed to be more like a barrier was around the area that kept most of the light out, or most of the darkness in.

She closed her eyes for a moment, hoping to find some strength in the dark behind her eyelids.

>>>A mill yeah. A mill yeah<<<

Amelia's eyes sprang open. The voice, much clearer this time, had cut through the gabble in her head, and this time she had no doubt at all. It was Stelka.

With one last fluttery breath, she stepped forward through the arch.

The dark was cold on her skin, like a heavy fog. The small courtyard was empty, apart from a broken earthenware water pitcher half-leaning against the far wall. To her left was a narrow flight of stairs, which led into another alleyway, as dark down there as the night before a winter dawn.

Pulling her cloak closer about her, Amelia headed down the steps and along the dim alley with the dark, enchanted sky a strip of blackness overhead. Stopping and squinting, she tried to see the end of the lane. She couldn't. Either it was too dark to see that far, or there was no end to it. Endlessly long, and deserted.

Unless ... unless something was watching her from the doorways, stoops and windows that glared empty, like the eye sockets in a skull. Somewhere quite nearby, something fiendish let out a long, caterwauling cry, and further away came the sound of a scream. Then a laugh, long and insane, followed by some kind of moan.

She jumped at the sound of the sudden words. 'Ye look lost, wee'un,' a wheedling, rust-edged female voice said, from very close by. 'Are ye sure ye're no lost?'

Amelia tried to calm her breathing and her pounding heart. She felt sure that she must have screamed, just a little, but she couldn't remember doing it. 'I'm not lost,' she said, her voice weak. 'Thank you.'

'Well ye look lost. Are ye sure ye're no meant to be going home for ye supper? Ye ma would be waiting. Be a dreadful shame to keep ye ma waiting.'

'I don't have a ma,' Amelia replied.

The voice tutted. 'Shouldnae have told me that, wee'un. I might've taken pity, had I thought ye had a ma waiting at home wi' supper on the table for ye. But since ye donnae ...'

'I don't want trouble,' Amelia said, as strongly as her breathless state would allow. She peered into the blackness of the shadows, trying to see the face that belonged to the voice. 'I just need to see someone.'

'Is that right? Well, out with it, wee'un – who is it ye need to see so badly? I cannae make no promises, mind.'

'I've come to see Dorissa.'

There was a pause. When it next spoke, all the twisted playfulness had gone from the voice. It was now deadly serious. 'What do ye want with Dorissa, wee'un?'

'It's between her and me.'

The voice was stern. 'No yet.'

'Are you able to take me to her?'

'Give me three reasons why I shouldnae turn ye back.'

Amelia thought. 'I'll give you four. One, Dorissa and I are old friends. Two, Stelka is in danger. I'm sure you remember Stelka, who used to be Chief Navigator before everything changed. Dorissa is the only person I know who can help me find her. Three, if I find Stelka, I think I might be able to find my other friends, Tab and Torby. And four, I think Florian is behind all these disappearances.'

'Why didnae ye start wi' that one?' the voice said. 'Since ye make such a strong case, I figure I can take ye to see Dorissa. But be warned – ye'd best no be jesting me, wee'un.'

'I'm not, I promise,' Amelia said.

'Very well.' From the darkness of a stoop to Amelia's left, a figure began to emerge. Amelia found herself gasping, then trying to cover it. It appeared that the voice of the old woman belonged to a child.

Its grimy face was covered with sores, and large patches of its thin hair had fallen out.

'What's the matter, wee'un? Have ye no seen a Fallowclann before?'

Dumbly, Amelia shook her head.

'And ye call yerself a magician!'

'I haven't been a practising mag ... Hang on, how did you know I was a –?'

'Well ye're either a magician, or ye really are lost! And ye seem to know what it is ye're here for.'

The Fallowclann turned, raised both her stubby little hands as high as she could and snapped her fingers. In an instant the lane was lined on both sides with the sickly glow of lamps on tall poles. Amelia gasped. The two rows converged far off in the distance. It seemed that the laneway really was endless.

'How does that work?' she said. 'The edge of Quentaris is less than a hundred feet in that direction, but this street is ... is *forever* long.'

'Ye're a slow learner, and that's for true,' the Fallowclann said. 'These days there's more magic in this wee lane than in all of Quentaris. Florian and his soldiers wouldnae dare come down here. I'll bet they wish they'd thrown us all over the side when they had the chance. Come on, wee'un, best ye hurry along wi' me, before someone less friendly spies ye and figures ye'd be good eating. Och, donnae look so terrified – I'm jesting wi' ye!'

'I'd rather you didn't,' Amelia said as the child with the old woman's voice began to lead the way between the endless lines of wan lamplight.

They travelled for what felt to Amelia like an awfully long time. In the lamp-lit street, the sounds of cruel, raucous laughter drifted about, mixed in with cries and calls. As they walked, Amelia noticed that most of the windows they walked past were completely dark, like almost everything else in Skulum Gate. But once in a while they would pass a window with some light behind it. Unlike the pale light from the lamps overhead, the light within these windows was weak, but warm, like a small flame. A candle, perhaps, or an oil-burning lamp.

'Someone's home,' she said as they passed one of these, but the Fallowclann didn't respond.

Still they continued on. The buildings were so similar – made more so by the darkness – that after a while Amelia began to wonder if they were walking in a huge circle, and passing the same windows all over again.

'Are we nearly there?' she asked the Fallowclann eventually.

'Aye, best ye donnae ask me that again, wee'un,' the old child-woman said.

'Sorry. It's just ...'

'We're here.' The Fallowclann stopped before a small doorway, which was shrouded in shadow. Through the window beside the door Amelia saw some of the weak but warm light she'd seen earlier.

'This is where I'll find Dorissa?'

The Fallowclann nodded, and pointed. 'In ye go, then.'

'You're not coming in with me?'

'Nae, I'll no come in. Me and Dorissa are no the best of friends.'

'Really? But she's ... well?'

'In ye go,' the Fallowclann said again, nodding towards the door. 'It'll no be locked. Not for yeself.'

'Will you wait out here for me?'

'So I can walk ye back? Are ye daft in some way? It's no hard to find ye way out!'

'I see. Well, thanks for bringing me down.'

The Fallowclann gave a half-hearted shrug, turned and headed back the way she'd come.

Taking a deep breath, Amelia put her hand on the door handle. It was so cold against her palm, and it tingled with frustrated, fermenting magic. 'Courage, Amelia,' she whispered. She twisted the handle, and with a clunk, the door swung open on creaky hinges.

The room was almost completely bare. The walls were white, but grimy and empty. The light within the room came from a single candle burning low in a large rack-like candelabrum in the corner. The candelabrum had once contained row upon row of candles – hundreds of them – but now there were barely a dozen or so left unburnt. The hundreds that had burnt out were now nothing but deformed globs of melted wax in their holders. Apart from the candelabrum, the room contained nothing but a bed, with a chest at its foot.

A very small, very old woman with long, white hair lay in the bed. The tissue-papery skin of her face was starkly pale against her plum-red dress, which had the remains of some tattered embroidery and beading still attached to it. She turned her head as Amelia opened the door and looked in.

'Yes, child?' the old woman said.

'I'm ... sorry,' Amelia stammered. 'I think I'm in the wrong room.'

'Who are you looking for?'

'I'm looking for Dorissa. She was ... she's a magician.'

'Only for a little longer,' the woman replied. 'Amelia, it's me. I'm Dorissa.'

Amelia frowned, and took a step closer. 'Is it ... No, it can't be ...'

'I've changed, haven't I?' Dorissa said. 'It's all right – you can say it.'

'Then yes, you've changed. A *lot*. When I last saw you, you were ...'

'Larger?'

'I was going to say younger.'

'It's this place, Amelia. It's Skulum Gate. We age faster here. See that?' Dorissa said, pointing with her eyes at the remaining candles. 'That's all I've got left.'

'What do you mean?'

'When the last candle burns out ...'

'No!'

'Yes. So you'd best talk fast.' Dorissa struggled to sit up, and Amelia rushed over to help her. 'Amelia, you shouldn't have come. You're in great danger. And staying here for a few moments will take days, perhaps even weeks or months off your life. So please, Amelia, say what you came to say and leave.'

'I don't understand.'

'Amelia, when Florian came to power, he knew that he needed to keep some magicians around, but

only those he could control, like Anira, or those that would be too obviously missed.'

'Like Stelka.'

'Yes, like Stelka. But he couldn't be seen to be killing off all the other magicians, so he gave us our own place ... this place, Skulum Gate. But it was enchanted, and our process of aging has been sped up. One thousand candles, they gave each of us. Yes, they burn slowly, but it's still not enough. And some burn faster than others.'

'Can't it be stopped?'

'You want to stop magic of this kind?' Dorissa's clear blue eyes filled with tears. 'If only I knew how. The street outside that door was once filled with people like me, magicians you would have known. Escalayn, Angard, Aylia, all bedridden now, like me.'

'Not dead?'

'Not yet, but it won't be long. Died of old age, Florian will say.'

'What about the baby-woman who showed me here?'

Dorissa sniffed. 'Moreon?'

'That was *Moreon*? She was one of my tutors for a while! I should have picked the voice. Why didn't she recognise me?'

'She probably did, Amelia, despite the disguise. Down here we get used to seeing people looking older than we remembered them. But she's most likely ashamed, and wouldn't have wanted to be recognised by you. There is a handful of Fallowclann in Skulum Gate. They dabbled in crooked magic a while back, and turned back part of the ageing process, but they went too far. They could go back to the outside world, but they'd be considered freaks. They'd never survive, especially with Florian at the top of the pile. And not just Florian – the other one.'

'Janus?'

'Yes, that's him. He knows far more magic than he lets on.'

'He's just Florian's chief advisor,' Amelia said.

'Is that what he calls himself? Well.' Dorissa snuck a glance at the candle. 'My dear Amelia, you really should tell me what you came for. I wouldn't want you to come to any harm.' She patted the side of the bed. 'Sit.'

Amelia sat. 'Something terrible's happened,' she said. 'They've taken Stelka.'

Dorissa nodded, and patted Amelia's hand. 'Yes, I know.'

SACRIFICE

The dark, glassy orbs hung in the water, their pale gaze fixed on the scout-pod and its four occupants.

'There are so many of them,' Tab murmured. 'What do we do now, Verris?'

'We need to speak with them.'

'Are these black things the Yarka themselves?'

Verris shook his head. His eyes were fixed on the orb directly before them. 'No, they live *in* those things. I think.'

'And what do they look like?'

'Like that,' Danda said. She was facing the other way, and Tab and Verris turned to follow the direction of her gaze. Shadowy figures were moving through the water. They were semi-transparent, like krill, but about the size of a large cat. Their antennae streamed behind as they propelled themselves through the thick water with impossible speed, and their eyes glistened blackly as they swept closer. There were twenty of them, perhaps more, and they swarmed around the pod. Then, one by one they settled on the deck and the railing, their heads moving from side to side as if they were watching Tab and her companions with first the right eye, then the left, then the right again.

'Aren't they going to say anything?' Tab said under her breath.

'They *are* saying something,' Danda replied. 'You can't hear them?'

'No. What does it sound like?'

'Listen,' Verris said. 'It's a bit like the sound of bubbles, only very high-pitched.'

Tab listened. For a while she heard nothing, but then, gradually, she began to hear the language of the Yarka.

'They're asking by what magic we've been able to come here,' Danda said.

'And what have you told them?' Verris asked.

'I've told them nothing. I'm simply the interpreter. What would you like me to say?'

'Explain that we have magic that allows us to come underwater without the need for air. But don't let them know that even we don't understand that magic,' he added.

There was a moment of quiet as Danda spoke in the high, bubbling voice. Then, after the Yarka had replied, she turned back to Verris.

'They say that they don't mean how did we come to be in the water – they want to know how we came to be in their *world*,' she said with a wide sweep of her arms.

'Tell them that we came through a vortex. Do they have a word for that?'

'I'll work something out,' Danda replied. More bubble-speak followed. 'Now they want to know what we want.'

'Tell them that we would like to buy icefire from them.'

'You want to just come out and say it?' Danda asked. 'No ... getting to know them? No exchange of gifts?'

'The gifts come later,' Verris said, and Tab saw his eyes go to Torby, just for a moment.

'Very well.' Danda returned to her translating, but something she said made the gathered Yarka stir from the railing and deck like seagulls rising for a morsel of food. 'They didn't like the part where I mentioned icefire,' she explained.

'Perhaps we should have worked up to that,' Verris said. 'Very well, apologise for my haste. Tell them that we mean them no harm, but that we wish to come to an arrangement that benefits all of us.'

Danda spoke, and a moment later came back with a reply. 'They wonder why you've come to them for icefire,' she said. 'They said that they have no icefire.'

'Are you sure you translated it properly?' Verris asked. 'The orders were very clear – we were to trade with them for icefire. Perhaps you got the word wrong.'

'No, I didn't get it wrong,' said Danda irritably.
'I made no mistake in the asking, and I made no
mistake in the hearing. They were quite clear – they
don't have icefire.'

'I think I see the problem,' Tab said. She'd opened the book to the orders and was rereading them. 'It doesn't say icefire at all. It just says "gemstones". Our mission was to trade with them for their powerful *gemstones*.'

'Tell them that,' Verris said. 'Ask them what kind of gems they possess.'

After a period of conversation between Danda and the Yarka that seemed to Tab to go on for far too long, Danda turned back to Verris. 'They're pretty angry,' she said. 'But I've managed to keep them calm for now. They want to know why we want their fire-crystal.'

'Fire-crystal?' Verris snapped. 'Icefire? That means the same thing!'

'It might sound like it, but I'm assured that it's very different indeed,' Danda said. 'And they don't like to give up their fire-crystal easily. Without promising anything, they want to know how many stones we need.'

'Three.'

Danda communicated this with the Yarka. Then, after more discussion in the strange language: 'They're still not happy, but they are prepared to consider. They want to know what we've brought to trade.'

'You know what to tell them,' Verris said grimly.

'No!' Tab grabbed Verris by the arm, and the Yarka stirred again at the sudden movement. 'No, you can't let them have Torby!'

'Enough, Tab!' Verris said. 'Don't make this harder than it needs to be. Danda, tell them.'

As the message got through, the Yarka began to stir with excitement, and those on the deck began to skitter and sidle towards Torby, lying silent and wide-eyed on his side.

'Verris! You can't! There has to be another way!'

Verris' eyes were sad, and Tab felt sure that if they hadn't been submerged, tears would have been rolling from them. He took her arm and led her to one side, which seemed strangely unnecessary, considering that the Yarka couldn't understand what he had to say.

'Tab, we both know that there isn't any other way. They won't let us go unless we leave someone behind, in which case we'll all die. Even if they allowed us to leave, we couldn't return to Quentaris without these gems. If we did, Florian would have us thrown straight back over the side, and they'd send someone else down here with Torby. Besides, it says in those orders that Quentaris' future relies on us getting these gems.'

'But at what cost?' Tab asked. 'Are you sure there's no other way?'

Verris' gaze settled somewhere on the middle distance as he thought. 'Unless ...'

'Unless what?' Tab said. 'Verris? Have you had another idea?'

Finally Verris shook his head. 'No, Tab, I don't

think there's another way. I know it's a terrible price to pay, but we're in no position to argue. Our lives are forfeit, no matter what happens. I'm sorry, Tab.' He looked at Danda then and nodded once, while Tab felt her heart breaking.

In a moment the scout-pod was surrounded with swarms of the Yarka. The water was thick with them, swirling and crowding, their legs paddling madly, their antennae waving about and their eyes staring with glassy intensity.

'The gems first,' Verris said, and Danda translated.

The Yarka parted like a crowd would for a king, and two of the larger individuals turned and swam towards the nearest orb. They were briefly silhouetted against the light from the portal as they entered, and a short time later they reappeared, carrying between them a blue-green gem, brighter even than icefire, so bright that Tab had to turn her eyes away as it was carried forward.

'Here,' Verris said, opening the small wooden case. The Yarka lowered the gem into one of the little recesses, then turned and swam towards another of the orbs. As they went, Tab saw that the orb from which the gem had come was now dark, with no light at all visible from within its portal.

The two Yarka were back with another gem, leaving the second orb dark and empty. As they went for the third, the Yarka nearby began to bustle and fidget, as if their impatience would spill over.

'Tell them to wait,' Verris growled to Danda.

The third gem was arriving now, and Tab felt dread rising within her as it was lowered into the case. She saw Verris close and latch the lid, leaving a thin crack of glowing turquoise along the edge. The dread continued to rise when the Yarka moved like a clot towards her friend Torby, and she choked back her cry and turned away. Whatever they were going to do, she couldn't bear to watch.

'Wait.' Even underwater, Verris' voice was full of

stern authority. 'Tell them to hold back.'

Danda translated the command, and the Yarka hesitated.

'Tell them to come right away from the boy. Quickly. There's been a change of plan.'

The Yarka drifted as Danda interpreted, and swarmed forward a little closer as she reached the end of the translation.

'Assure them that there's no treachery here,' Verris said. 'Tell them that there's to be a substitute. They can't have the boy.'

'Who, then?' Danda asked, fear tinging her voice.

'Not you, Danda. Tell them.'

Danda spoke in her bubbling, squeaking way, and the Yarka hovered uncertainly.

'Verris, what are you doing?' Tab asked quietly.

'It's all right, Tab. Danda, tell them that they can take me.'

Tab's mouth fell open. 'What?'

'Tab, don't say anything. Danda, tell them.'

'Are you sure?' Danda asked.

'Tell them. If they need convincing, tell them there's more meat on me than there is on him anyway.'

Danda turned back to the Yarka and told them what Verris had said. As one, and without hesitation, the creatures surged forward with bubbly squeals of delight, and then, flashing past as fast as minnows in a pond, they set upon Verris, knocking him to the deck. Their semi-transparent bodies swarmed and pulsed over him, and then they were lifting him, carrying him out over the unplumbed depths below towards the nearest empty orb.

'Verris!' Tab cried, and Danda stood with her, clinging to her arm.

The Yarka pulsed around the figure of Verris as he was passed end-on through the dark portal. Then, in huge numbers, they began to pour in, following him into the orb.

'Your spell,' Danda said quietly to Tab. 'Say what you have to say and get us out of here before the rules are changed again.'

* * *

Tab cried all the way back to Quentaris. The pod rose slowly into the early morning sky towards the great hulk of the city above. Somehow – she wasn't at all sure how, with the sobbing – she'd been able to read the diagrams and incantations in the book, and had managed to choke out the sounds needed to get the pod moving up through the water towards the underside of the nearest pockmark in the ocean's surface. Then, in a strangely un-wet kind of way, the pod broached the surface and continued to rise towards the dark hulk of Quentaris.

'Are you all right?' Danda asked Tab, who was by now sitting quietly against the railing with Torby's head on her lap.

Tab sniffed back her tears. 'Verris was the nearest thing to a father I ever had,' she said. 'Like he said, we did a lot together. Once I even locked him in a fortified room while the city guard were coming.' She smiled weakly. 'I did help him get out, though. He thought that was so funny. I think he admired me for it.'

'He was a good man,' Danda said.

'Good isn't even close,' Tab replied. 'To do that for Torby ...'

'It was a noble thing to do.'

'He'd be dead by now, wouldn't he?'

'I don't know ...' Danda said tentatively.

'I know he would be. You won't make me feel worse by saying that he is.'

'Then yes, I expect so.'

Tab couldn't speak.

AMELIA SEES SENSE

'Stelka may not be easy to find, Amelia,' Dorissa said. 'If she is trying to mind-meld with you as you say, then she's using magic that is quite new to her.'

'And to me,' Amelia said. 'But I thought you might be able to teach me.'

Dorissa shook her head. 'I can't mind-meld, Amelia. I'm not sure that I can even show you how to do it. Besides, it's not something you can just learn, like juggling.'

Amelia smiled, remembering how she'd used almost those exact words herself.

Dorissa went on. 'But there is one fact in your favour.'

'What's that?'

'Stelka has reached you, so your chances of reaching her are good.'

'So can we try?'

Dorissa smiled. 'Of course we can try, but as I say, I can't promise anything ...'

Amelia nodded. 'I'm ready.'

'And I don't want you to feel discouraged if it
doesn't work straight away.'

'I'm ready.'

'Then close your eyes and do as I say.'

* * *

Stelka's voice was horribly harsh in Amelia's head,
but she persisted, shifting the sounds around like
boxes in a room until they made more sense and
order.

>>>Amelia? How you found me?<<<

>>>Dorissa<<<

>>>Dorissa? Dorissa alive?<<<

>>>Yes, she's alive, in Skulum Gate<<< Amelia
replied, choosing to leave it at that. The rest could
wait. >>>Where are you?<<<

>>>They came and take me different place. Bad
magic is come soon<<<

>>>What kind of bad magic?<<<

>>>Bring fire-crystal from Yarka<<<

>>>They're getting icefire?<<<

>>>No! Fire-crystal! Different! Very powerful!
Darker magic. Stronger magic<<<

>>>Magic that you know how to do?<<<

>>>Yes! No more vortex with this magic<<<

>>>Well, that's good ... isn't it?<<<

>>>Gives power to city can appear to kill and
steal and disappear very fast<<<

>>>Can appear to kill and steal?<<<

>>>No, I said wrong. Can appear, then kill and steal, then disappear<<<

>>>So with this magic Quentaris can appear in a world, take what it wants, kill who it wants, and disappear without waiting for a vortex?<<<

>>>Yes! Yes!<<<

>>>Stelka, it's very simple, isn't it? You can't do this. You can't let Florian have this magic!<<<

>>>Torture. Terrible torture<<<

Amelia had no response. She couldn't imagine what kind of torture could be dealt out to Stelka. Enough to make her do this dreadful thing? It must have been truly horrifying. Physical torture? No, Florian wouldn't stop at that. He'd use the magicians that he'd corrupted, working in darkly enchanted cells to torture Stelka in the worst ways their magic could conceive.

>>>Stelka, do they have the fire-crystal yet?<<<

>>>Not yet. They say come soon. They send party to Yarka<<<

>>>A party?<<<

>>>Verris in charge<<<

>>>Verris is alive?<<<

>>>I was with surprise too<<<

>>>Who else is in this party?<<<

>>>Verris leads party with Navigator and<<<

The connection was gone. The voice had vanished.

>>>Stelka?<<< Amelia shouted in her mind.

>>>Is the Navigator Tab? Stelka!<<<

The voice was still there after all. >>>Caught me melding with her. Me let slip who it was. Was accident. Feel so bad, want to fix but can't. Am bad person now. You should not meld me any more<<<

>>>Stelka, who else is in this party?<<<

>>>Navigator, interpreter and someone must leave behind. Someone weak<<<

It was as if Amelia's veins had suddenly filled with ice. >>>Torby? They've taken Torby with them? They have, haven't they?<<<

>>I go now<<< Within Amelia's mind, she heard Stelka's voice crack. >>>I hate what I become. Don't look for me<<<

This time the connection really was gone, and Amelia felt Stelka's presence drain away like water from a broken pot.

She opened her eyes. Dorissa's room had gone blurry, and she wiped her tears away with her sleeve. 'They took Tab and Torby,' she said. 'And they've got Stelka doing terrible, terrible magic.'

Dorissa reached out and took Amelia's hand. 'I'm sorry,' she said. 'I'm sorry you went to all this trouble to find me, only to leave with bad news.'

'Is there any way to find her? I mean, to find where she is?'

Dorissa shook her head. 'Unless Stelka wishes to be found, she won't let it happen. She holds powerful magic, but she's been to the evil side of magic now, and will never come back. How could she? How could she come back and face everyone now?'

Amelia bowed her head and let the tears flow freely. 'So that's it, then? Verris is gone, Tab is gone, Torby is gone, even Stelka is gone, or she might as well be.'

'If they do their job well, Verris and Tab will be back,' Dorissa said. 'But they might be changed forever – it's impossible to know.'

'And Stelka?'

'Stelka is strong, but stubborn. If she says she won't return, then we should believe that to be true. I'm sorry.'

'And Torby?' Amelia asked in a low voice. 'How about Torby?'

'I'm sorry.'

* * *

Amelia strode from the archway without any disguise. The make-up was wiped unevenly from her face, the clothes discarded back in the endless lamplit street of Skulum Gate.

Reaching the end of the lane, she turned left and marched towards the palace, barely noticing how bright the light seemed after the dimness of Skulum Gate's heavy winter sky.

'Hey! You're back!' Philmon dropped down off the ledge he'd been waiting on and trotted alongside Amelia. 'How did you go?'

'They took Tab. And Torby. Verris is alive. But Stelka is ...'

'What? Dead?'

'No, but she might as well be. She's gone over with them.'

'So where are Tab and Torby?'

'On a mission. They were press-ganged. But Torby's not coming back,' she said, furious tears stinging her eyes.

'So where are you going now?'

'To have words.'

'Whoa! Whoa!' Philmon grabbed her. He gripped both her shoulders and turned her to face him. 'Now it's time for *you* to see sense. What can you hope to achieve by going up there?'

'I'm angry, Philmon,' she snarled. 'Can't you see?'

'Yes, I can see that. So can the rest of this street.

You almost knocked over a stall back there. You need to calm down.'

'How can I possibly calm down?'

'Listen, the play starts in a couple of hours.'

'I can't go to a play now!'

He shook his head. 'No, listen to what I'm trying to say. If you go up to the palace, even if you get to see Florian – which I doubt – he'll either laugh at you, or worse, you'll be sharing a cell with Stelka, or sharing the ocean with whatever lives down there. Besides, by now Florian would be up on Tarquin's Hill in his fancy tent, eating until he's sick. So instead, we go back to your place, you clean yourself up, we go to the play, and if you must confront Florian, you do it there, on your terms.'

'What do you mean, on my terms?'

'I mean you confront him in front of hundreds of his own citizens, on his birthday. What's he going to do then?'

Amelia sighed, and looked back over her shoulder towards the playhouse. Then she glanced in the direction of the palace. Finally she nodded. 'You're right. You're right. Nothing can be fixed by going to the palace.'

'Good. So, let's go and get ready for the play.'

FONTAGU PRESENTS ...

With a loud rattle of chains and a heavy grinding groan, the rock opened. The scout-pod, still operating entirely under the magic that Tab had invoked, adjusted its course slightly and headed into the cave-like door that had appeared in the cliff that comprised part of Quentaris' hull.

Tab barely noticed. She was still weeping for Verris as she half sat, half lay beside Torby.

'Tab. We're back,' Danda said, placing her hand on her shoulder.

'I don't care,' Tab replied, but she looked around anyway. The pod had risen through the tunnel, coming to a stop beside a kind of pier, inside a barn-like room. In the gap between the edge of the pod and the pier she could see the tunnel stretching down, and beyond that the blue of the ocean, far below. The ocean that Verris was still in.

Two men stood waiting, both large, muscled and armed. One looked like he might have had some troll blood in him, several generations back, judging by his wide jaw, low forehead, and stocky legs. The other was an albino, with pure-white hair, freckled skin and pink eyes. Tab didn't recognise either of them, until they spoke.

'You're back,' said the albino, in a coppery voice. 'Did you get what you went for?'

'In the chest,' Tab spat. 'Your filthy jewels are in the chest.'

'And the book? We will need the book back. Can't leave orders like that lying around the place,' the albino said.

'Hold on, where's the pirate?' asked the troll, frowning as his eyes scanned the pod. He pointed at Torby in disbelief. 'You idiots! You left the wrong one behind! You were meant to leave the weakling behind and bring the pirate back!'

'Is that how you saw it happening?' asked a familiar voice.

Tab supressed a surprised squeal of delight as she saw Verris appear from the shadows behind the two men. He was armed with a long piece of timber, which he brandished like a quarterstaff.

The men turned, gaped, and drew their swords.

'What's this treachery?' said the albino. 'Did you get the gems like you were told to?'

'Oh yes, they're there all right, in the case, just as Tab said.'

'And the Yarka let you just ... have them, did they?'

'Not exactly. The thing is, they're rather more accommodating than we're led to believe, those Yarka. Very big on honour.'

The men glanced at one another, confused. 'What are you talking about?' the half-troll asked.

'Well the thing is, they're actually quite trusting. You see, if you promise them something, they tend to take you at your word.'

'What's he going on about?' the albino asked his partner.

'Let me make it simple for the less intelligent amongst us,' Verris said, his eyes twinkling. 'I offered myself up to the Yarka instead of the boy. They were happy with that arrangement. After all, there's a lot more meat on me than there is on him. But then I got to thinking, there must be someone up in Quentaris who has more meat on him than there is on me.' Verris' eyes settled on the half-troll. 'You're a big chap, aren't you?'

'You're not serious,' the albino said.

'Oh, I'm quite serious. Fortunately the Yarka knew I was quite serious as well, because they took me at my word when I promised them a feast before the sun went down tonight.'

'You're wasting time, pirate. Frankly I don't care what promise you made to that seafood buffet down there, but we've got work to do, so get out of the way.'

'Oh, but I *do* care about the promises I make,' Verris said. 'It's just the way I was raised.' Then, with a movement so fast that it was a blur, he sprang forward, disarmed the half-troll with a twist of his quarterstaff, sending him staggering backwards towards the pod. The half-troll's footing slipped, and he fell between the railing of the pod and the side of the pier, struggled for a moment as he continued to slip, then slid screaming down the tunnel that led to the open air, and the enormous fall to the ocean's surface.

'The thing is,' Verris said as the albino cowered at the edge of the pier, 'the Yarka can get awfully hungry. It can be weeks or more between meals, and sometimes, when they do get to eat, they like a second helping.'

With a whimper, the albino dropped his sword and bolted from the room.

Tab leapt out of the pod and threw her arms around Verris. 'How did ... Where were you?'

'I rode up on the underside of the pod. I wanted my appearance to be a surprise.'

'But the Yarka ... They took you into their big round black thing.'

'I negotiated, like I said. They really are very honourable creatures, once you talk to them as equals.'

'Talk to them?' asked Danda. 'How did you talk to them?'

Verris shrugged. 'You don't follow the pirate career path for as long as I have without picking up the odd foreign word here and there.'

'So you can speak Yarka? Why didn't you say so?'

Verris smiled. 'I wouldn't call myself fluent. I could say what I needed to to escape, and that's about it. Besides, let's face it, Danda, if you'd been sent all the way down there only to discover that your presence wasn't actually required, you'd have been pretty annoyed, wouldn't you?'

'I'm pretty annoyed now!' she replied. 'And to be honest, I think I'd quite like to go home, if that's all right.'

Verris smiled. Then he took both her hands in his. 'Danda, you have played your part, and you've played it well. Quentaris might not be ready to thank you just yet, but given time it will. Go home now. And I ... we thank you.'

As soon as Danda had gone, Verris stepped down into the pod, which rocked gently under his weight. He bent and picked up Torby. 'I think we're late for a night at the theatre, after a quick stop at the palace. There might be one or two generals locked away down there who are looking for a phalanx of militia to lead.'

'Where are we going to find the phalanx of militia?' Tab asked.

'They're locked up in the cell next to the generals.' He shook his head and chuckled. 'What kind of idiot keeps officers and men in a place where they can work on a plot together?'

'An idiot like Florian?' Tab suggested.

'Precisely that kind of idiot. Come on, Tab, let's hurry.'

* * *

The audience was in, and Fontagu was nervous. And these were more than just first-night nerves – these were serious frightened-of-doing-something-that-might-get-me-killed nerves.

He pulled the side-stage curtain apart slightly. The footlight candles were lit, and over in the royal box the refreshments were being laid out, ready for Florian and his party to arrive.

'Mister Wizroth.'

Fontagu turned. A boy in a dress was standing there, biting at his thumbnail.

'What is it, Lindo?'

'I'm scared.'

'Of course you are – you're a terrible actor.'

'Do you really think so?'

'Of course, but it's too late to be thinking about that now. We've prepared as well as we can, and now it's time to put it all together. Yes?'

'Yes sir. But what if I mess up my lines?'

'I've no doubt you all will, but we'll just do our best,' Fontagu said, checking the royal box again. There was some movement at the back, followed by a fanfare from a trumpeter. The audience turned to welcome Florian, who squeezed into his seat and offered a bored wave.

'This is it, Fontagu,' he whispered to himself. 'Time to be glorious once more.' Then he let out a long fluttery breath and wiped his clammy palms on his thighs, before turning to Lindo. 'Go and tell the others to get ready – the Emperor's just arrived. Go!'

The boy hurried off, and Fontagu put his hands to his face, closed his eyes and took another deep breath.

'Fontagu?'

'I've told you, we're as ready as we can be! Now go to the others and tell them –'

'No, it's us, Amelia and Philmon.'

He turned around. 'I'm sorry, children, I thought you were someone else.' He took both Amelia's hands in his own. 'Oh, thank you for coming. Is everything all right? Did you find the person you needed to find in Skulum Gate?'

Amelia blinked, nodded, and looked at the floor. 'Yes,' she said quietly.

'From your eyes I see that it was bad news?'

'Not the best. Listen, Fontagu, I just want to wish you the very best for tonight. We both do.'

'That's right,' Philmon agreed.

'Thank you, children. Well, I'm glad you could make it. I don't ... I don't suppose Tab ...?'

Philmon and Amelia shook their heads.

'Oh. Well then. Never mind,' Fontagu said with a tight, grim smile.

The stage manager had come over while they were speaking. He tapped Fontagu on the shoulder. 'We're all ready to go, Mister Wizroth.'

'Thank you. And Florian knows when to come backstage for his ... his cameo?'

'He does, Mister Wizroth.'

'Good, good. Well, children, your stall is waiting. And I do hope you enjoy the play. Oh, and there's one more thing. Could you look after Fargus? I can't risk having him run across the stage in the middle of the play.'

'Of course,' said Amelia. 'We'll collect him on the way. Good luck, Fontagu.'

Fontagu winced. 'You can't wish someone good luck in a theatre, Amelia!'

'Oh. Sorry. Then ... bad luck, I ... I suppose.'

'That's better,' Fontagu said, relaxing slightly. 'Enjoy the play.'

After Philmon and Amelia left, Fontagu looked out from the side of the stage once more. There was Florian, and Janus, and several other important people and their servants, already stuffing their faces.

'Strength, Fontagu,' he whispered. 'Time to do something noble.'

* * *

'These are good seats, aren't they?' Philmon said. He looked down on the cheap-ticket holders, standing in a crush in the main part of the theatre.

'There had to be some advantage to being friends with Fontagu,' Amelia said bitterly. She glanced across at an empty chair. 'Tab should have been there, though.'

'I know. But you need to focus on what you're going to say to Florian in front of all these people. Are you still going to do it?'

Amelia felt the anger still burning in her chest. 'Oh yes,' she said. 'Definitely.'

'Oh, here we go,' Philmon said as Fontagu emerged from the side of the stage and walked to the centre. 'He looks nervous.'

'He should be.'

The noise from the audience settled as Fontagu

stood there, waiting. When there was complete silence, he raised his chin, extended one of his arms, and bowed low towards the royal box. 'My lord,' he said.

Florian nodded once and stuffed a bunch of grapes into his mouth.

Fontagu straightened and faced the audience. 'Dear friends, I am Fontagu Wizroth the Third, and tonight I have the very great honour of directing and performing my own modern adaptation of the greatest of all Quentaran classics, *The Gimlet Eye*. This performance was commissioned as a birthday gift from the city of Quentaris to its leader, Florian the Great, Supreme Emperor of Quentaris. As befits the occasion, later in the performance there will be a surprise guest appearance, which I feel sure you will enjoy.'

Fontagu hesitated, then cleared his throat. 'Before we begin, I wish to dedicate tonight's performance to a wonderful and most esteemed person, the like of whom I have ever known, and may never know again.'

Amelia glanced in Florian's direction. The horrid little oaf was smiling smugly around at the crowd.

Fontagu went on: 'The performance you are about to see will be in the honour of my very dear friend, Tab Vidler, who yesterday disappeared without trace, in most suspicious circumstances. We hope for her safe return, but are prepared for the very worst.' He turned towards the royal box, and the no-longer-

smiling Florian. 'My lord, we give you, in three acts …
The Gimlet Eye.'

'Go Fontagu!' Amelia muttered.

'Brave or stupid?' Philmon said.

'Quite a bit of both.'

It came as something of a surprise to Amelia to see how good Fontagu actually was. The other performers ranged between fairly good and outstanding, but Fontagu's class was clearly evident. Whenever the crippled carpenter Robar came onstage, it was plain to see that the actor playing him was truly in his element. His voice was strong and emotive, his lines delivered with perfect timing and enunciation, and Amelia found herself looking forward to his every reappearance.

Philmon seemed to be finding the performance just as engaging, for at some time in the second act, just as the villagers were preparing to go out hunting for the monster, Amelia stole a glance at him, and saw that his eyes were wide. He was sitting slightly forward, and his lap was empty.

'Philmon! Where's Fargus?' she whispered.

'What? Oh! Oh no!'

'Where did he go?'

'I don't know!' Philmon said, looking under his chair and around the stall. 'I'll have to go and look for him!'

'Wait,' said Amelia. 'Let me try something.' Then she closed her eyes.

'What are you doing?'

She didn't answer him. She was too busy trying to use her fledgling skill to find the mind of Fargus.

Shutting away the strange garbled noise of the hundreds of minds in the playhouse, she went looking for a little, doggy mind. It took some doing, but eventually she found Fargus. At least, she was pretty sure it was him, sniffing around at the base of a chest. Off to one side she saw some backstage props that she recognised from the play, and a short distance away she could hear Fontagu delivering some of Robar's lines.

She suddenly felt a pain in her backside, and a voice she didn't recognise said, 'Out of the way, mutt

– I'm in a hurry.'

Fargus whimpered and looked up. Through his eyes, Amelia was shocked to see a stocky, red-headed man limping across to a large table strewn with props. He was carrying something in his hand, but with his back turned to Fargus, it was impossible for Amelia to know what it was.

Then he was turning around, and Amelia saw what it was he was holding. It was a sword.

She left Fargus' mind with a start. She was breathing hard as she said, 'He's backstage.'

'I'd better go and get him,' Philmon replied. 'We can't have a dog running across –'

'Not the dog,' Amelia said. 'The man. The red-headed man with the little knife. And a sword. Rendana is backstage. I can even smell the tigerplums.'

Philmon frowned at her. 'What's he doing?'

'I don't know. But I'm sure he's up to no good.'

'He's not backstage any more,' Philmon said, nodding towards the royal box. Amelia looked, and saw Rendana standing at the back of the stall. He caught Janus' eye, and nodded.

'Something's not right,' Philmon said. 'I'm going back there.'

Amelia stood up. 'Then I'm coming with you.'

As they reached the backstage area, they almost ran headlong into Fontagu, who had just come behind the curtain at the end of a scene. 'What are you two doing here?' he asked crossly. 'Florian will be here for his cameo in a moment, and then I'm back on. It's a very quick turnaround for the next scene.'

'Fontagu, something's wrong,' Philmon said.

'I know, I know, that idiot murdering the part of Darmas Girth has just botched his last line, I swear it.'

'Actually, it's not that —' Amelia began to say, but she stopped as Florian and a couple of his courtiers arrived.

'Wizroth! Explain yourself!' Florian blustered, standing up close to Fontagu. 'What do you mean to do, dedicating this play to that Vidler child? It's Our birthday. Ours!'

'Steady, Amelia,' Philmon said under his breath, as she stiffened.

'I ... I meant no disrespect, my lord,' Fontagu stammered.

'You might have thought it was noble and brave, but We thought it was rather foolish, in the scheme of things,' Florian said. 'But we can talk about your so-called future later. For now, We need Our costume.'

'Over here, my lord,' Fontagu said, taking a cloak from a hanger nearby. 'It should fit ... We thought it would be quicker and easier if your costume just slipped over your very fine, very elegant clothes, which do befit your greatness and your —'

'Oh, do shut up, Wizroth,' Florian said, slipping

the cloak on. 'Now, where's Our sword?'

'Here, my lord.' Fontagu handed him a wooden sword, painted to look silver.

Fontagu swung it about as if he was preparing for a real duel. 'Yes, this will do nicely,' he said, and Amelia had to bite her tongue again. Florian had never been much good with weapons when he was the spoilt nephew to the Archon, and now as a spoilt Emperor he was probably just as useless. 'And Actor, remember to let me look good before you kill me.'

'Of course, my lord,' Fontagu replied.

'Now, when is Our cue?' Florian looked around smugly, making sure that everyone had noticed his use of a real acting word. 'I believe We go on from stage left, is that right?'

'Stage left is right. I mean ... stage left is correct, my lord,' Fontagu said, picking up his stage sword from the props table. He attached it to his belt, momentarily confused by the buckle. But then it was on, and he gave his head a little mind-clearing shake and looked at Florian, who suddenly appeared to be struggling not to vomit. 'Ready?'

'Of course,' Florian replied. 'Why wouldn't I be?'

'Um ... Very well, my lord. Break a leg.'

'Yes, well let's hope not.'

'No, of course.'

From the side of the stage, Amelia and Philmon watched Fontagu make his entrance. He walked up to the boy playing Robar's wife Sarad, who was in the middle of a long speech about how much she was missing her dead friend the hunter.

As Robar, Fontagu stood there, listening to his wife weep. Then, as she paused, he stepped towards her, taking her hand in his. 'Why harken thee to the early morn and list to hear the voice of lovers?' he recited, his voice bold and clear.

'O Robar, deride me not this never-fine day, for my heart grows sullen-headed with worrisome affront,' Sarad replied, pulling her hand from Fontagu's and turning away to gaze offstage.

Fontagu stepped towards her again, speaking to her back. 'Even with birdsong I heard our casement squeak, and coming hither I spied thee, your face with torment razed, while I had erstwhile slumbered within our wedding casket.'

'But lo, who from afar approaches?' Sarad said.

'That's my cue,' Florian said, and clearing his throat, he stepped into the glow of the footlights.

Even from backstage, Amelia heard the crowd gasp as they recognised Florian. Then came the tittering. He'd come in on the wrong side of the stage, and Robar and Sarad were facing in the opposite direction.

Florian waited until they'd noticed and had turned to face him. He hesitated, then began his lines, but without much confidence. 'Greetings. I am Calran, a wandering hawker, out to do great harm and no good. I have seen your fine animals and this, your lovely wife, and wish to take them all for myself, O lame and blind carpenter.'

'You insult me with your devilish handsomeness and your working legs and eyes,' Robar replied. Judging from the way he winced, Amelia could tell that Fontagu was hating these clumsy lines he'd been forced to say, but he pressed on regardless. 'Lame and half blind I might be, good sir, but I will not stand idle by while you take all my fine animals and this wife to whom I'm married.'

'Then shall I fight you for them, and her?' Florian asked.

'If you wish,' Fontagu retorted, drawing his sword. 'Have at you!'

The swordfight was in full swing when Amelia remembered. As she watched Fontagu and Florian move about the stage with clumsy stage-fighting, she glanced across at the royal box. Janus and Rendana had remained there, Janus sitting, the red-headed man standing, and as she looked at Rendana, what she'd seen through Fargus' eyes returned. Could it be? No, of course not. She must have made a mistake.

'You fight ever so well for a humble hawker,' Fontagu was saying.

'Thank you. And you are quite good for a blind, lame carpenter, but it would still take a stroke of very good fortune for you to defeat me.'

At that moment, Florian 'tripped' over a stool in

the middle of the stage and fell onto his backside.

'A stroke of good fortune like that?' Fontagu said, standing over Florian and raising his sword, ready to run the hawker through. 'Now you die!'

'Stop!' Amelia screamed, leaping forward onto the stage. 'Fontagu, don't!'

The crowd gasped at the interruption. So did the actors. Florian looked up with an expression of horror and fury, but Fontagu simply stared in surprise.

'Amelia! What are you doing?'

'Get off!' Florian hissed. 'He was about to kill me!'

'Yes, he was,' Amelia said, reaching up and taking the sword from Fontagu's hand. 'With this.'

'It's a stage sword, you silly girl,' Fontagu said. Then he groaned. 'Oh, now you've gone and ruined everything!'

'A stage sword? Are you sure?' With a sharp downward thrust, Amelia jammed the tip of the sword into the stage. It quivered there for a moment, its point buried deep in the boards.

'What? I don't ...' Fontagu fumbled. 'It was meant to be a stage sword. It was always meant to be a stage sword, my lord, I swear it!'

His face pale, Florian had climbed to his feet. He shrugged the costume from his shoulders and stepped closer to the trembling Fontagu. 'What treachery is this, Actor?'

Fontagu fell to his knees. 'My lord, I wish I could explain, but ... but I can't. I truly believed that to be a stage sword, not ... not a real one.'

'Of all the people I might have expected to attempt an assassination, I would have hoped it to be someone a little more dignified than ... than *you*. Get up, you disgusting wretch. You'll be swinging from the nearest yardarm before the sun rises again.'

'How about Janus – are you going to hang him as well?' Amelia asked in a clear, strong voice.

There was absolute silence in the playhouse as Florian turned slowly towards Amelia. 'I *beg* your pardon? You would dare to insult my dearest friend?'

'Your dearest "friend" tried to have you killed. The only thing is, he was too cowardly to do it himself.'

'That's a very serious accusation,' Florian said with a scowl. 'What proof do you have?'

'Ask him,' Amelia said, nodding towards the royal box.

All attention turned to Janus, but he simply laughed. 'What? The girl's mad! She's making up fairytales!'

'If I'm making up stories, why will the guards find your servant carrying a stage sword instead of a real one? I'll tell you why – because he substituted a real sword for the fake one. You wanted Florian dead, but you would rather have seen a Simesian actor commit the crime and pay the price.'

'Dead? Why would Janus want me dead?' Florian asked. 'He's my friend!'

'He's not your friend. He wants your throne. Why else would he have brought Kalip Rendana and his men aboard from Unja Ballis? Why else would he have arranged a part for you in this play, where you could be stabbed, in public, by someone who could then be executed? You're the last in the line. It was the Archon, then you, then ... no one. So who would have been the next ruler of Quentaris? Verris? Not when he hasn't been seen for months. So it would have been him – Janus! Janus the Cowardly.'

'This is preposterous,' Janus said, laughing again. But this time there was a lot less conviction in the laugh. 'It's all completely fanciful nonsense!'

'Let's find out,' said Florian. 'Guards, seize them, and bring them down here. Bring both of them – Janus and the Unja.'

Half a dozen soldiers overpowered Janus and Rendana and brought them down to the stage. They were held firmly by the arms while Florian strutted along in front of them, enjoying his extended time on the stage. 'Well then, let's see this sword,' he said.

One of the guards drew the sword from Rendana's belt and handed it to Florian, who frowned at it, turned it over a couple of times, then spun to face Janus. 'Traitor,' he said, and with a sudden lunge he stabbed a surprised Janus through the heart.

The crowd gasped, and Janus looked as though he might faint, but when Florian withdrew the sword, there was no mark, no blood, no wound in Janus' chest. 'It's a stage sword, just like the girl said,' Florian announced, dropping the weapon on the boards. 'Take them away!'

The audience broke into applause as Janus and Rendana were led to the side of the stage, down the wooden steps and into the crowd. They parted to let the prisoners through, and as they passed the applause changed to hissing and booing.

Meanwhile, Florian stood in the centre of the stage and raised his arms, waiting for silence. 'There is no place in Quentaris for treachery such as this,' he began. 'And as you have seen, under Our rule justice is meted out swiftly and fairly. These traitors will pay with their lives.'

'I do trust you're going to judge yourself by those same standards, O great emperor,' boomed a voice from the wings.

Everyone looked. Then a ripple of amazement went through the audience as Verris stepped forward, with Tab at his side. Verris, who most Quentarans believed to be dead.

'Verris!' said Florian. 'You're back!'

'Yes, we're back.'

'Did you get –'

'Yes, we got your gems from the Yarka,' Verris answered. 'Everything went ... swimmingly.' He paused to smile at his own joke. 'There was a slight complication, however.'

'A complication? Whatever do you mean?'

Verris stepped behind the curtain, and was back a moment later with Torby in his arms, still silent and motionless.

Florian looked confused. 'Is that ...?'

'Yes, it's the child you were prepared to sacrifice for the sake of your greed.'

The crowd murmured, but Florian looked around with an amused expression. 'Everyone's gone mad! Sacrifice? Seriously, Verris!'

Verris shook his head. 'Just so everyone knows, Florian was prepared to send four of us to trade with the Yarka. But only three of us were meant to come back. Show them, Tab.'

Tab held up the book of orders. 'It's all in here,' she said.

'You shouldn't still have ... But we needed icefire,' Florian tried to explain. 'The city needs icefire to ... to survive.'

'That's true, but it wasn't icefire we were sent to get, was it?' said Verris. 'It was something rather different.'

'Fire-crystal,' said a new voice, and Amelia felt her heart leap as Stelka stepped out of the shadows of the curtains. She was without her jewels and finery, her hair had been hacked in a short skullcap, her face and arms were bruised, and her eyes were tired and sad, but it was undeniably her.

Amelia rushed forward and threw her arms around Stelka, who drew her breath in sharply.

'She's been through a lot, Amelia,' Verris said. 'Be gentle.'

Florian was clapping slowly. 'A touching display,'

he said, 'but could we get on, do you think? You see, I'm ... We're rather curious. We'd like to know more, so if you're all so very clever, pray tell us all about this so-called "fire-crystal".'

'It's needed for a particular kind of spell,' Stelka said. 'While I've been in the cells, your men ... Wait, you know this already, so I might as well put it this way: you have been putting me to work finding the vortex that would take us to the Yarka. And once you had enough fire-crystal gems —'

'Three, in fact,' Tab interjected.

'— I was to go to work on this new spell, the Spell of Infinite Transition. It is the spell which will allow Quentaris to simply appear in one world, stay for as long as it needs to, then leave just as easily, without needing to call up or search for a vortex.'

'But surely that's a good thing!' Florian said, with a little too much enthusiasm.

Verris shook his head. 'Not when your intention is to sweep in, plunder whole worlds at will, then leave before they have time to respond. That, my friends, is piracy of the first order. And believe me, I would know.'

Florian looked around, desperation now beginning to spread across his face. 'This is all utter speculation!'

'No,' said Verris. 'It's all true. And if you'd like to go on denying it here, in front of so many of your loyal, long-suffering subjects, it will only look worse for you when you face trial.'

'Trial? *Trial?* You can't try me! This is mutiny!'

'What would it be if I killed you, right here, right now?' Verris asked.

'It would be high treason, of course, and no one would deny it! High treason!'

'I agree. And if I were to throw you to the Yarka?'

'The same! Treason! Murder!' Florian was turning one way then the other, his face red, his eyes bulging with anger. 'He's gone mad! The pirate has gone stark, staring —'

'And what if I suffocated you with a pillow – would that be murder as well? Would that be treason?'

'Of course it would!' Then Florian's face changed, just a little. 'Why do you ask, Verris?'

'Isn't that what you did to our venerated Archon not so long ago?'

Florian was suddenly lost for words. His mouth opened and closed like a fish beached on the sand.

'You seem to have lost your ability to speak, Florian,' Verris said. 'But Janus was there, wasn't he? He saw you do it. And I'm sure that he'll admit that when he is offered a reduction in his sentence for telling us what he saw. And he'll also testify that you were acting on the old prophecy which states that to assume power is to lead, but to take power is to rule.

It's the very prophecy he was seeking to honour by arranging your murder today.'

'But my uncle was dying anyway!' Florian suddenly blurted. 'I was simply speeding up the horrid, painful process! That's not murder – that's mercy!'

'You killed him, Florian,' Verris said. 'You killed him. Which makes you guilty of high treason. Guards, take him away.'

'They're not your guards to order around!' Florian screamed as two armed men stepped forward, caught him under the armpits and dragged him offstage.

'Perhaps not, but in a matter of moments my newly-released generals will be here with the militia you locked away in your rat-infested dungeons. I have to say, Florian, I wouldn't want to be one of these guards when those boys arrive. Soldiers need to fight – it's what they do – and they've been itching for a scrap, sitting down there with nothing to do for

several months. You know, your guards might be just what they've been dreaming about. Fresh meat, so to speak.'

The nearest guard had gone rather pale. 'We'll ... we'll do whatever you say, sir,' he stammered. More guards nodded in agreement. 'I never liked him anyway!'

'Let me go!' Florian shouted as he was dragged away. 'Verris, we can work this out! Can't we talk about it? Oh, this is so unfair!'

'Oh, stop your whining,' Verris said. Then he muttered, 'That boy never did like to lose.'

THE AFTER-PARTY

'How did you get to Stelka?' Amelia asked, pouring another thickleberry wine for Verris.

'It was her,' he replied, nodding at Tab, who was reclining against a pile of stage curtains. 'All those guards that came aboard with Rendana back on Unja Ballis – well they don't just work out the front of the palace, you see. Once he'd told Florian about the Yarka and their fire-crystal, Rendana could do more or less whatever he wanted. He had his men in all sorts of key positions. And the thing is, being newcomers, they weren't ready for some ... experimental magic, let's say.'

'You don't think I spend my entire day convincing farmers to sing to shickins, do you?' Tab said. 'Just because I work on a farm doesn't mean I don't try to keep my skills up to date.'

'And this experimental magic involved what?' Philmon asked.

Tab shrugged. 'Oh, you know, just a bit of mind control ...'

'And when that didn't work, the sleeper hold is always a good backup plan,' Verris said, smiling.

'I've got a question,' Fontagu said. 'The pillow over the face of the Archon – was that just a lucky guess?'

Tab shook her head. 'Just because Torby can't speak doesn't mean his mind isn't working. And as Amelia knows, if you know what you're doing, you can get into the strangest places with your mind.'

'Maybe I'm drunk, but I don't understand,' Fontagu said.

'Torby was there,' Tab explained. 'He saw Florian do it. And he heard Janus encourage him, and quote the prophecy. But then, he went back to how he'd been, all ... blank. He was still very fragile, and he couldn't take the horror of seeing someone killed in front of his eyes like that. But then, in a funny sort of way, he told me, once I bothered to go into his mind and ask the right questions.'

Fontagu shook his head in confusion. 'No, I still don't get it. I *must* be drunk.'

'I doubt it,' said Amelia, re-corking the bottle and placing it on top of a prop chest. 'Thickleberry wine doesn't have any alcohol in it.'

'It doesn't?' Fontagu said, staring suspiciously at his drink.

'So what happens now?' Philmon asked. 'Can Quentaris go home?'

Stelka shook her head. 'The reformed council

will have to decide what we do with the fire-crystal, but if we do invoke the Spell of Infinite Transition, we'll put laws in place that allow us to only use it for peaceful purposes.' She leaned forward. 'What Florian didn't know was that there is a lot of work to be done between getting the fire-crystal and invoking a spell as big as that. I mean, what kind of mess would we end up in if any old person off the street could grab a gemstone and start throwing spells around willy-nilly?'

For a moment, it seemed as if Fontagu was going to choke on his wine.

'And that is why, as of half an hour ago, the curse over Skulum Gate began to lift. We magicians are going to need as much help as we can get.'

Amelia's eyes were wide. 'Will all the magicians from Skulum Gate come back?'

'We hope so, Amelia,' Stelka replied. 'We can't restore life, but we are fairly sure we'll be able to reverse the artificial aging process.'

'And Torby?' Philmon asked.

'He has to start healing all over again,' Stelka said. 'Seeing the Archon die was such a terrible blow for Torby, especially since he had to carry that knowledge around. But we hope for the best.'

'That's good,' Amelia sighed. 'Poor Torby. Imagine that, solving a great mystery without having to say a word.'

'A very great mystery indeed,' Verris said.

There was a long pause around the stage as the friends drank, and thought, and reflected.

Suddenly the silence was broken by the sound of a sob, and everyone looked. Fontagu was crying into his hands. 'Oh, my big break, my great opportunity to make it back into the industry, and the third act is interrupted by high treason. Oh it's true – my career is cursed.'

'Well look at it this way,' Verris said. 'Everyone present tonight will remember your production of *The Gimlet Eye*.'

'I suppose so,' Fontagu agreed, sniffing loudly.

'And with a couple of notable exceptions, no one went home disappointed.'

'But what if the treason and the attempted murder are the only things they remember?' Fontagu wailed. 'How about the acting, the direction, the writing, the stagecraft? From what you saw, how did it stack up? Be honest, now.'

Amelia was the first to speak. She stood up, walked across the stage to where Fontagu sat with his elbows on his knees, his head hanging low. She wrapped her arms around his shoulders and hugged him. 'Fontagu Wizroth the Third, tonight, when I heard you dedicate that play – Florian's *birthday play* – to Tab, I thought you were very brave.'

He looked up at her with bloodshot eyes. 'Really? Brave?'

'Oh yes, Fontagu. Brave, stupid, and truly magnificent.'